PREMEDITATED INTENT

David Brunelle Legal Thriller #13

STEPHEN PENNER

ISBN: 9780578918587

Premeditated Intent

This is a work of fiction. Any similarity with real persons or events is purely coincidental. Persons, events, and locations are either the product of the author's imagination or used fictitiously.

Joy Lorton, Editor.
Cover design by Nathan Wampler Book Covers.

PREMEDITATED
INTENT

"Premeditated" means thought over beforehand.

When a person, after any deliberation, forms an intent to take human life, the killing may follow immediately after the formation of the settled purpose and it will still be premeditated. Premeditation must involve more than a moment in point of time. The law requires some time, however long or short, in which a design to kill is deliberately formed.

State of Washington
Pattern Criminal Jury Instruction 26.01.01

CHAPTER 1

"That's a lot of blood."

And it was. Blood on the floor. Blood on the walls. Blood on the refrigerator, and the oven, and the dishwasher. Blood on the counter, and the toaster, and the faucet. Even blood on the ceiling. But mostly blood all over the murder victim lying at the feet of King County homicide prosecutor David Brunelle.

"Astute observation," replied Seattle Police Detective Larry Chen. "You should be a detective."

The hard line of Brunelle's lips curled up slightly, and he shook his head. "No, thanks. I'd spend all my time at murder scenes trying to keep blood off my shoes."

Chen offered back a dark grin of his own. "Yeah." He glanced down at the horror in front of them. "That would suck."

The victim was an African American female, mid 30s, average height, medium build. She was dressed for a night in: cotton pajamas and a terrycloth robe. The pajamas had been pink and the robe had been white, before both were stained red and black with large swaths of the aforementioned blood.

There was a myth that dead people looked like they

were just sleeping, that somehow a sense of peacefulness shrouded every corpse with a final gift of serenity. That might be true for some people, Brunelle supposed, like people who died in their sleep, so they were found in bed, under the covers, with their head on a pillow, maybe a sleep mask over their lifeless eyes. But it was definitely not true for the bodies Brunelle saw. Those bodies looked like the nightmares people woke up screaming from. There was nothing peaceful or serene about a woman sprawled across her kitchen floor, her own blood covering everything around her, her arms and hands and fingers still extended in her futile attempt to escape her fate.

The other way Brunelle knew the victim wasn't just sleeping was that it was really very loud in that apartment right then. Not quite loud enough to wake the dead, apparently, but certainly loud enough to wake the merely sleeping. While the murdered woman lay motionless on the floor, the apartment around her bustled with activity. For her, it was the end of living; for everyone else there, it was making a living. Brunelle paid his rent standing over dead bodies at 2:00 a.m. And he wasn't the only one.

Technicians from the medical examiner's office were beginning their preliminary documentation of the body before prepping it for transport to the morgue. Forensic officers were placing evidence markers next to every object which might have even the slightest chance of being important later, then stepping back to photograph all of those objects. Two junior detectives were walking slowly through the apartment, hands in their pockets, scanning every inch of wall and floor to see if there were any clues the forensics team had overlooked. A handful of patrol officers were milling about, awaiting tasks from the detectives, radios crackling with static and unrelated callouts for everyone to hear. Somewhere in the distance a baby was crying. And on the couch by the front door, another 30-something African American woman was sobbing onto her hands.

Brunelle glanced around the packed apartment. In addition to the sights and sounds, there was the smell. Not anything as poetic as the 'smell of death'—that would come later at the morgue when the M.E. made the first incision into the already decaying body. No, it was the simple but overpowering smell of blood. Fresh blood. A lot of blood. Metallic and burnt, it filled the nose and penetrated the sinuses. Brunelle took one last look at the body, tugged at his nose to blunt at least some of the stench, then tapped Chen on the arm to follow him as he stepped the few feet from the kitchen to the crying civilian.

"I'm Dave Brunelle," he introduced himself, "from the King County Prosecutor's Office. This is Detective Larry Chen. Can I ask your name?"

It was nicer than, 'Who are you and why are you crying?' which is all he really wanted to know right then. Two in the morning was definitely a vinegar time, but civilians usually needed honey.

The woman looked up and wiped her nose with the wad of tissues she'd had her face buried in. "Valerie," she sniffled. "Valerie Jones. I'm Amelia's neighbor. I'm the one—" she stifled another sob "—I'm the one who found her."

Brunelle would have said, 'found *the body*', but then he didn't know her. 'Amelia'. He'd have to remember that.

"What happened?" Chen asked.

Valerie looked up at the patrol officer who was standing a soft watch near her. Not keeping her from leaving exactly, unless she actually tried to leave before the detectives could talk to her, then definitely keeping her from leaving. "I already told the officer."

Chen nodded and offered understanding eyes. "I know. And thank you. But I need to hear it from you directly. I'm the lead detective, and this is my investigation. It's important I learn as much as possible directly from each witness."

And you'll be asked this question a dozen more times before the case is done, Brunelle knew. But he kept his mouth shut and allowed the witness to give her statement.

"Amelia and I are friends," Valerie started. "We've both been living here for a couple of years now. We moved in about the same time. We both have kids about the same ages, and we help each other out, you know? She watches my two- and three-year-olds sometimes; I watch her three-year-old and her baby sometimes."

"Sure, sure," Chen encouraged. But he allowed her to continue in her own way.

"We watch out for each other too," Valerie continued. "Watch each other's apartments, make sure nothing shady is going on, and also make sure we aren't dating the wrong type of men, you know what I'm saying?"

Brunelle knew exactly what she was saying.

"So, we might babysit for each other if one of us had a date," Valerie explained, "but then we'd check the guy out before and after and make sure he wasn't trouble. Neither of us were looking for drama. Just looking for companionship. We don't need some guy stepping out on his wife, or some fool running drugs who's gonna bring the cops around."

She stopped and took a moment to look around. "I mean, no offense," she added.

"None taken," Chen assured her.

"Cops suck," Brunelle agreed. "Keep going."

Valerie gave a puzzled frown at Brunelle's comment, but heeded his instruction. She'd stopped sobbing. Focusing on answering questions did that. It would work in the courtroom, too, when the time came for Valerie Jones to tell the jury what she was about to tell Brunelle and Chen.

"I had a date tonight," Valerie went on, "so Amelia was watching the kids. The plan was for the kids to spend the night at her place, in case my date went late, you know?"

Brunelle knew that too.

"Plus, you don't wake up a toddler once he's asleep," Valerie warned, "unless you want to spend all night trying to get him back to sleep. So, I was just gonna check in with Valerie, tell her how the date went—not so good, by the way, which was why I was home kind of early."

"Sure," Chen acknowledged again.

"But as I was walking up to her apartment," Valerie's expression started to shadow the tragedy that unfolded around her when she got back from her date, "I knew something wasn't right. I could hear the baby crying. Babies cry, right? But not like that, and it was too loud. I shouldn't have been able to hear it as far away as I did. When I got to her door, I saw it was open a crack. I could hear the baby just wailing right through the crack in the door, and that just wasn't right. Her door should have been closed and locked, and that baby shouldn't have been crying like that."

Brunelle wondered absently if he could get Valerie qualified as an expert on how babies should cry. He didn't give voice to that thought either. "Then what?" he prompted.

"I pushed the door open and called out, 'Amelia?'" Valerie recounted, "but there was no answer. And that baby's cries were even louder inside. There was no way Amelia could have ignored crying like that, even if she wanted to. So, I walked all the way in and that's when I saw her—"

The sobs came back quicker than Valerie expected, catching in her throat and pouring out of her mouth and nose.

"Oh my God," she gasped. Then the rest of the story spilled out as fast as it could to avoid getting cut off by the wave of new sobs Valerie was barely holding off. "I saw her foot, just barely sticking out from the kitchen. I saw the blood on the floor. And I knew. I just knew. But I didn't know for sure, you know? So I had to look, and I looked, and oh God, there was blood everywhere, and Valerie was just lying there, and I guess I should have helped her, but that baby was crying, and there were three other kids in the apartment, and I didn't know if whoever did it was still there, and so I just ran back to the bedroom, and I grabbed the baby, and I woke up the little ones, and I just told them to cover their eyes and pushed them out of the apartment and across the hall to my place. And I locked the door and called 9-1-1. And then I just waited until you all got here. And that baby never did stop crying."

Brunelle raised an ear to confirm. Yep, the baby was still crying somewhere not too far away.

"Did you see anyone else in the apartment?" Chen asked.

Valerie shook her head, and whimpered in the negative, her words overcome by those sobs she'd only barely managed to hold off.

"Do you have any idea who might have done this?" Chen followed up. "Jealous boyfriend? Maybe one of those guys she dated?"

Valerie shrugged. "I don't know anyone who would do

something like this." She dared a glance at the carnage in the kitchen. "Who could do this?"

That was the question. And it looked like they might already have their answer.

A patrol officer stepped over, hand still on his radio. "Detective Chen," he interrupted. "Sergeant Cooper just called in. He has a suspect in custody. Suspect's name is Harris, Kevin."

"Kevin?" Valerie looked up with wide eyes. Then her eyes narrowed again and cast downward. She nodded slowly. "Yeah. Kevin could have done this."

CHAPTER 2

The rain sputtered onto Brunelle's windshield as he drove up Sixth Avenue to the Seattle Police Department's downtown headquarters. The rain wasn't heavy enough to bother turning on the wipers—that would have just smeared everything and made it even harder to see the lane dividers already lost in the wet reflections of the streetlights. He needed new wipers. It was Seattle; he always needed new wipers.

They drove separately from the crime scene. Chen got to park in the underground lot and take a nice, dry elevator up to the interrogation room to meet Sgt. Cooper and the suspect. 'Kevin Harris'. He'd have to remember that too. Brunelle had to park on the street and enter through the main lobby. Fortunately, there were actually free parking spots on the street at three in the morning. Unfortunately, the rain had picked up. He turned up the collar of his coat, lowered his head, and hurried from his car door to the precinct door.

The parking spots were free, but they weren't very close, so by the time Brunelle finally ducked into the lobby of the police headquarters, his shortly cropped hair was soaked, and he could feel the rain seeping through his coat onto his shoulders.

"Mr. Brunelle?" the single patrol officer at the reception desk called out. An easy deduction. Guy in a suit showing up at three in the morning looking somehow both focused and a little lost. Obviously, a prosecutor. "Detective Chen is waiting for you."

A metal door on the side of the lobby opened remotely with a buzz and a clank. No one came out to escort him inside. One of the benefits of being on the same team with the cops. He crossed the lobby, pulled open the heavy door, and lumbered inside, his shoulders getting even wetter from the movement. He fought off a shiver and marched toward the interrogation room. He knew the way.

Chen was waiting for him, standing outside the observation room next door, and connected by a two-way mirror.

"Cooper just parked," Chen informed him. "He'll be upstairs in a minute with the suspect."

Brunelle gestured toward the interrogation room. "Hopefully, this goes well, and I can graduate him from suspect to defendant."

"Agreed." Chen nodded. "In the meantime, make yourself comfortable."

It didn't sound like a joke, but it was a joke. There was scant comfort to be found in the observation room, just a couple of backless stools set up near the two-way glass. He would have liked some instant coffee and maybe a microwave to heat up the water, but he supposed the 'ding' from the timer might alert the suspect that someone was watching from the other room.

Sgt. Cooper opened the door to the interrogation room

and escorted Kevin Harris into the chair opposite Chen. Well, more like pushed him down into it, probably more forcefully than necessary, mean-mugged him, then strutted out to leave Chen to his work. A jarringly quick moment later, Cooper opened the door to the observation room and joined Brunelle inside.

"Oh, hey," Cooper said upon seeing him. "You're here for the show too, huh? Prosecutor, right?"

Brunelle smiled slightly. He glanced performatively at his suit, tie, and drying trench coat. "What gave it away?"

"Yeah, you do look the part," Cooper responded. He pulled up the stool next to Brunelle. There wasn't anywhere else to sit anyway. "But I'm pretty sure we've met before."

That was likely, even probable. Cooper looked to be about 50, with gray stubble on the sides of his head and a thick white moustache. That suggested they had both been doing their intertwined jobs for a couple of decades. At least one of Cooper's cases must have come across Brunelle's desk somewhere along the way. He couldn't really place the face, but the name was familiar.

"Yeah, I think so," Brunelle decided to agree. "I'm sure I've seen your name on some reports. Probably sent you a subpoena or three."

"Or twenty, probably," Cooper laughed. "Who can keep track, right? Bad guys keep doing bad shit, good guys keep putting them away for it, am I right?"

Brunelle didn't really think of it like that, but Cooper wasn't wrong. "I hope so." He nodded toward Chen and Harris. "Let's see if this bad guy can help us put him away."

They turned their attention to the happenings on the other side of the glass.

"Mr. Harris," Chen began, "I'm Detective Larry Chen. Can I call you Kevin?"

Harris shrugged and looked away. He would have crossed his arms, but Cooper had left them handcuffed behind his back.

Harris was probably in his early 40s, a little older than his victim. He was big, at least six feet, and probably pushing 250 pounds. He had light brown skin, dark black hair, and red-rimmed mean eyes. Not angry, Brunelle decided, *mean*. Cruel. But then again, Brunelle knew he might just be seeing what he wanted to see. Either way, Harris already seemed like a jerk.

"Great," Chen continued. "You can call me Larry."

"Man, I ain't calling you anything," Harris shook his head and looked away. "The only thing anybody's calling anybody is you calling me a lawyer."

And end scene. Brunelle frowned. A suspect could say just about anything and the interrogator could keep going, keep pressing and probing and looking for that weak spot that would lead to the confession that became Exhibit A at the trial and sentencing. But there was one magic word that stopped the interrogation: 'Lawyer.' That was the end of it, legally speaking. Chen could go on. He could ignore Harris's request and press ahead with the interrogation, but it wouldn't matter. Every syllable out of Harris's mouth from that moment forward would be suppressed by the judge for violating Harris's constitutional right to an attorney.

"You sure about that?" Chen tried. "This is your one chance to tell me your side of the story."

Brunelle's frown deepened. Even that ploy was risky. A suspect could take back their request for an attorney, of course, but it had to be completely unambiguous. And it had to be initiated by the suspect. Chen was allowed to clarify, Brunelle supposed. There was always some gray area. Brunelle made his living in the gray areas.

"Am I sure?" Harris laughed. "Uh, yeah. I'm sure, Larry. I'll tell my side of the story to the public fucking defender. In the meantime, how about you let me go or take me to my cell? It's the middle of the fucking night, and I just want to go to sleep."

He didn't say 'back' to sleep, Brunelle noted. But that was all the statement analysis he was going to get to do. The interrogation was over. Everyone knew it.

Even Chen. He pushed himself back in his chair. "Fine." Then he motioned toward the mirror. "We'll be happy to take you to a cell."

"That's my cue." Cooper jumped off of his stool.

"Too bad it was so quick," Brunelle complained. "I wish he would have given us at least something incriminating."

"Oh, he did," Cooper beamed as he opened the door. "I got a full confession from him at the scene. I'll tell you all about it when I get back."

CHAPTER 3

"He confessed?" Chen's expression was a combination of surprise, relief, and irritation.

"I guess so." Brunelle shrugged. "At least that's what Cooper said—just before he walked out."

"That would have been nice to know before I started my interrogation." Chen shook his head. "Still, nice exit line."

"Got my attention," Brunelle agreed. "He said he'd be right back after he stuffed Harris in a cell."

Chen frowned. "Just enough time to make some crappy instant coffee. Shit, Dave, I'm getting too old for this."

"No, you're not," Brunelle laughed. "You don't want some boring nine-to-five life. You can stop staying up all night at murder scenes when you're dead. Also," he held up his own nearly finished mug, "the coffee is pretty good."

Chen nodded. "Yeah, you're right. On both counts."

Sgt. Cooper reentered the observation room, a big grin under his mustache. "Well, that could have gone better, huh?" he asked jovially. "No worries, though. Like I told Mr. Prosecutor Man, I got a full confession out of him at the scene."

"Brunelle," Mr. Prosecutor Man reminded him.

"Right," Cooper pointed a fat, weathered finger at him. "Mr. Brunelle, the prosecutor man. Anyway, yeah, Harris confessed. We're good."

"What did he say?" Chen asked.

"He said he did it," Cooper answered. When Chen's stony expression didn't lighten, he added, "You mean, like details?"

"Details would be nice," Brunelle put in. "Juries like details."

"So do detectives," Chen said. "And supervisors."

Cooper put his hands up defensively. "Okay, okay. I got it." He patted his uniform's chest pocket. "I took notes. It will all go in my report."

"It better," Chen warned.

"Of course, it will," Brunelle soothed. "But why don't you give us a dry run now? I'd love to charge this guy as soon as the courthouse opens. A confession would help me significantly. Right now, the only evidence I have that he's the murderer is that you arrested him for it, and that's not evidence of anything."

Cooper gestured toward the Formica table at the side of the room. "Sure thing, Mr. Brunelle, sir. Let's grab a seat and I'll tell you exactly how it went down."

Brunelle didn't need Cooper's official report before he filed charges, but he at least needed the information therein. He offered his stool to Chen, who declined it. So, Brunelle and Cooper sat down, and Cooper extracted his field notepad and flipped to the last page with writing on it.

"Here we go." He said. "Harris, Kevin. Murder One. Suspect contact."

"You didn't happen to audio-record it, did you?" Brunelle interrupted. He suspected the answer but held out some small hope that Cooper quickly extinguished.

"Sorry, sir. It was a pretty volatile situation. I'm not going to stop in the middle of a takedown of a murder suspect to pull out a tape recorder."

Brunelle frowned but nodded. He could understand that. And so would the jury. "Fine. It's not required. You can tell the jury what he said. It's just nice to sit in the courtroom and hear the defendant confess to the murder in his own voice."

"I'll do you solid," Cooper assured him. "This isn't my first rodeo."

"What did Harris say?" Chen interrupted with an impatient slap on the table.

"Right." Cooper refocused his attention on his notepad. "These are my notes, so it's a little choppy. Victim was girlfriend. Ex. Still hooked up sometimes. Went there after midnight. Wanted drugs, sex, money. All three."

"All three?" Brunelle asked. "He said all three?"

Usually one of those alone was enough motive for murder.

"Yeah," Cooper nodded. "I remember because I was like, 'Man, isn't one of those enough? All three?' and he said, 'Yeah, all three'."

Brunelle nodded. "Okay." He didn't mind having an embarrassment of motives.

"Right, so anyway." Cooper looked down at his notes again. "Um, all three. Babysitting. Told him to leave. Didn't have any drugs or money. Wasn't going to have sex. Kids there. Got angry. Pushed her. She slapped him. He punched her. She started screaming. Told her to shut up. Grabbed a knife from the counter. She grabbed for it. Blacked out."

"Blacked out?" Brunelle repeated. "Who? Her or him?"

"Um, him," Cooper answered.

"You sure?" Chen asked.

"Yeah, yeah." Cooper tapped his notepad. "They always say that. Right when they get to what they did, they say they blacked out. Right?" he asked Brunelle.

Brunelle frowned and nodded. "Yeah, I've seen that before. Total bullshit. Juries see right through it. Well, usually. I might have to call a psychologist to explain that's not how blackouts work. You don't stab someone a dozen times during a blackout. Still, I would have preferred some details on the actual killing."

"Would you also have preferred the murder weapon?" Cooper grinned. "'Cause I got that too."

"You recovered the murder weapon?" Chen's eyes widened. "Where?"

"How?" Brunelle changed the question. How was going to be more important than where, at least to him and the defense attorney who would undoubtedly try to suppress all of this from the jury.

"On his kitchen counter," Cooper answered Chen's question first. "It still had blood on it. We got there quick. He didn't even have time to clean it."

"How?" Brunelle repeated. "Did you get his permission to enter the house?"

"Yeah, of course," Cooper half-laughed. "Everything was by the book. Caught the murderer, got a confession, recovered the murder weapon. All in all, a pretty good night."

"Not for the victim," Brunelle pointed out.

Cooper just shrugged.

"Okay, by the book, right?" Brunelle wanted to confirm. "So, you Mirandized him before he confessed, right?"

"Of course," Cooper assured.

"Did you use a form," Brunelle clarified, "or just read from your field card?"

"Again, counselor, I was in the middle of arresting a murder suspect," Cooper answered. "I wasn't going back to my patrol car to get a form for him to sign. I read him his rights just like they're printed on my field card. He acknowledged them and agreed to speak with me."

"Understood," Brunelle said. But he still had to prove the advisement of rights happened. "Was there another officer there who can corroborate?"

Cooper frowned at the obvious suggestion his word might not be enough, but he bit his tongue. "Yes. Officer Thompson was with me. He witnessed everything."

Brunelle relaxed. "What about the search of the house? Did you advise him of his *Ferrier* rights?"

"Ferrier?" Cooper cocked his head.

"*State v. Ferrier.*" Brunelle felt a tick of panic. "The State Supreme Court case that says in Washington you have to advise someone of their right to refuse or limit a search?"

"Oh, yeah, that." Cooper pointed that thick finger at him again. "Um, yeah. I mean, he said the knife was in the kitchen and he gave me permission to retrieve it. I didn't really search, exactly."

Brunelle frowned. *Ferrier* didn't require written warnings, but it had specific language that was required in the warning. "What exactly did you say? Did you tell him he could refuse the search, or limit it, or end it at any time?"

Cooper shrugged. "I asked him where the knife was, and

he told me I could get it."

Brunelle's frown deepened.

"I mean," Cooper tried, "I think I could see it from the doorway. That's plain view, right? I can grab it if it's in plain view."

"I don't think that's how plain view works," Brunelle sighed.

"Open view?" Cooper suggested.

Brunelle shook his head.

"Are you saying I should've gotten a warrant?" Cooper huffed.

"I'm saying a warrant would have been better," Brunelle answered. "A warrant is always better."

"Taking. Down. A. Murder. Suspect," Cooper repeated in defense of his actions.

Brunelle thought for a moment, then shrugged. "It doesn't have to be perfect procedure," he allowed. "I can probably argue some limited exception to the warrant requirement."

"Plain view," Cooper suggested again.

"Not from the front door looking inside someone's home," Brunelle knew. "But there are others. Exigent circumstances. Preservation of evidence. Inevitable discovery. I'll think of something."

Cooper smiled, but it wasn't warm. Again, that fat, pointy finger. "You do that, Mr. Lawyer. I did my job. Now, you do yours."

CHAPTER 4

In that job Brunelle was supposed to be doing, he split time between whatever courtroom he'd been assigned to for trial and his office on the sixth floor of the King County Courthouse. He was between trials just then, and needed to draft up some charging documents on the soon-to-be-filed case of *The State of Washington versus Kevin Harris*, so Brunelle crossed the marble-floored lobby to the courthouse's central elevator bank, pressed the 'up' button, and completed his morning commute to his desk.

Government offices weren't nearly as nice as the ones private lawyers had. They couldn't be. If they were too nice, the local politicians, on behalf of the taxpayers, of course, would complain about waste and excess and such. That meant yellowing paint on the walls, minimal décor, and furniture from the Clinton Administration. The boss called it 'utilitarian'. Brunelle called it a job. He wasn't trying to impress clients, and no matter how old the paint or the furniture was, he still had a view of Elliot Bay. Well, a peekaboo view now that the latest skyscraper had popped up between him and the water.

He sat down at his desk, happy to be back in the proverbial saddle. He'd just completed a short leave of absence that mostly consisted of a long trip to Europe with his girlfriend, the lovely and deadly Casey Emory, detective extraordinaire. Well, lovely and a detective anyway, but across Lake Washington at the suburban Bellevue Police Department, so a lot less deadly. Still, extraordinary, at least to him. It had been a nice trip. It was even nicer to be back where he belonged: a long row of government offices in a government building housing government lawyers. His people. Which reminded him.

He knocked on the office two doors down from his. "Welcome wagon. Are you new to the neighborhood, miss?"

Gwen Carlisle, prosecutor extraordinaire, looked up from her own aged desk, although her computer looked newer than Brunelle's, he noticed. They'd tried a couple of cases together when Carlisle was newer and working her way up from property crimes to violent crimes. Her new office confirmed she'd made it to Homicides. With Brunelle's mentoring, he liked to think.

"I've been here for a few weeks now, dumbass," Carlisle replied with a cock of her head. She looked the same as when he'd last seen her. Short blonde hair, sharp eyes, perfect suit. And a mouth like a sailor. "I moved in while you were off getting your shit together."

"My shit has always been together," Brunelle defended. "I just needed a vacation. Now I'm back and ready to prosecute me some murderers."

"Cool, cool," Carlisle replied with a nod. She gestured at the papers spread across her desk. "Me too."

Brunelle raised a finger in the air. "Speaking of which, can I run my latest case past my protégé?"

"Your equal?" Carlisle corrected. She took a moment to survey her own work, then let go with a sigh and leaned back in her chair. "Sure."

"Equal," Brunelle repeated as he sat down across the desk from her. "Okay, Equal, this was my callout last night. Victim was stabbed to death in her apartment. Multiple stab wounds and blood everywhere. Murderer caught within a few hours. Confession. Murder weapon recovered, still bloody."

"Her blood?" Carlisle raised an eyebrow.

"We'll have to get it tested," Brunelle conceded, "but I'm sure it will come back to her."

"So," Carlisle ticked the information off on her fingertips, "murderer in custody, full confession, murder weapon recovered. Sounds like a slam dunk. Are you really that rusty after one little vacation?"

"It was a long vacation," Brunelle replied. "And sure, big picture, it sounds great. But there are devils in the details."

"You know that's not the actual phrase, right?" Carlisle raised that eyebrow again.

"Did you understand me?" Brunelle asked.

Another sigh. "Sure."

"Then that's the phrase," Brunelle asserted. "Anyway, the confession wasn't recorded. He gave it to the arresting officer but then lawyered up when he got back to the station and Chen took a run at him."

"Okay, so it's a field confession. That'll hold up in court." Carlisle opined. "He Mirandized him, right?"

"Yeah," Brunelle confirmed.

"Any witnesses to the advisement?"

"A junior patrol officer present."

"Okay, so you'll have to call both of them to the stand at

the inevitable suppression hearing," Carlisle analyzed. "There's case law on that. If the defendant takes the stand and says the cop didn't Mirandize him, and you don't call the second cop, there's an adverse inference the first cop is lying."

"I'm familiar with the case law," Brunelle responded. "I'm just not familiar with the cops. I wish it had been a detective. A detective would have gotten it on tape."

"Chen didn't," Carlisle pointed out.

"Probably because the guy realized he should have kept his mouth shut on his way downtown," Brunelle suggested. "That's why they don't like field confessions."

"Still," Carlisle turned up her hands at him, "I'm not seeing any devils."

"The suspect didn't actually confess to stabbing her," Brunelle expounded. "He claimed a blackout."

"They all claim that." Carlisle laughed slightly and shook her head. "Man enough to kill a woman but not man enough to admit what they did."

"I'm not sure we need to bring gender into this," Brunelle straightened himself up. Then he frowned and looked at the ceiling. "Or is it sex? I get those confused sometimes."

"I'm sure you do." Carlisle shook her head at him. "I'll ask my girlfriend. You do the same. Then we'll compare answers."

"Double date?" Brunelle suggested.

"No way," Carlisle was quick to reply. "I don't want her thinking I have straight male friends. It would ruin my rep."

"You work in a prosecutor's office," Brunelle turned his own hands up. "Everyone is a straight male."

"Doesn't mean we're friends," Carlisle pointed out.

Brunelle didn't have a witty reply ready for that.

"You said something about a murder weapon?" Carlisle steered the conversation back to work.

"Right. Yes." Brunelle returned to his recitation of the case. "Recovered inside the suspect's home."

"Warrant?"

"Nope."

"*Ferrier* warnings?"

"Also nope."

"Ah," Carlisle steepled her fingers. "So, that's a devil. What did the cop say?"

"Plain view."

"From the front door?" Carlisle questioned. "Was it on the floor right there or something?"

"In the kitchen," Brunelle answered.

"Can you see the kitchen from the front door?" Carlisle asked.

"I haven't been out there yet," Brunelle answered, "but I doubt it."

"Yeah, that's definitely a devil," Carlisle repeated. "But if the DNA comes back to your victim, I don't see any judge suppressing that. Not in a murder case. Your cop probably should've locked the place down and gotten a warrant, but you don't want the evidence to disappear or degrade somehow."

"Yeah, that's what I was going to argue," Brunelle agreed. "For all my cop knew, the suspect might have had a roommate inside who was just about to do the dishes."

Carlisle tipped her head slightly. "Work on that."

"Yeah., I will." Brunelle nodded. "So, you want in? Like the old days? Brunelle and Carlisle against the world?"

"Carlisle and Brunelle," she corrected, "and no." Another gesture at the work piled on her desk. "I've got my own homicide caseload now, Dave. I think you can manage to squeak out a conviction with a confession and the murder weapon."

Another knock on Carlisle's door interrupted their conversation. It was Nicole Richards, the head paralegal for the homicide division. Tall, dark, and awesome. She looked shaken. "Dave?"

Brunelle's mind ran down a list of reasons Nicole would both look scared and be looking for him. Was he in trouble? Again? Did he do something to piss off the boss without even knowing it? Again?

"What is it, Nicole?" he asked.

"It's Larson," Nicole answered. "Jacob Larson. He's out. He got out a week ago."

"Out?" Brunelle's heart flushed with adrenaline, and not in a good way. A wave of memory and panic poured over him.

"We just got the notification," Nicole confirmed. "He finished his sentence. He's out of prison."

"Who's Jacob Larson?" Carlisle interjected.

Brunelle took a moment before he could speak. Then he explained. "He's the one defendant I think might actually try to kill me."

CHAPTER 5

"Only one?" Carlisle quipped. "I would've thought there'd be a long line of defendants wanting to murder you."

Brunelle didn't laugh. Neither did Nicole. She sat down next to Brunelle as he began to explain.

"This was a long time ago," he began. "Before you got to the office. I was still new to homicides."

"It was your first murder trial," Nicole recalled.

"Right. See, the problem with prosecuting murder in Washington," Brunelle explained what they all already knew, "is that you only get twenty years for it. Well, twenty to twenty-five, plus any weapon enhancements. But the point is, if you're young enough when you murder someone, you're getting out again. And that twenty years is on Murder One, premeditated. If it's Murder Two, intentional but not premeditated, then it's only ten to fifteen years. No weapon enhancement, ten percent off for good time, and credit for time served awaiting trial, and you could be out eight years after your conviction. For *murder.*"

"Okay, but no one gets the low end, and there's usually a weapon involved," Carlisle argued, "so it's more like you get out in fifteen years."

"And then you get even," Nicole chimed in.

Carlisle frowned. "Fifteen years is a long time. Prison changes people. We prosecute hundreds of defendants over a career. Maybe thousands. What makes this guy different? Why do you think he's going to kill you?"

Brunelle took a moment, remembering. "Because he said he would. And I believe him."

Carlisle shook her head again. "Who is this guy? What did he do? Who did he even kill?"

So Brunelle told the story. "He was this young punk. Twenty, maybe twenty-one. Wanted to be a tough guy. Was always going around picking fights. I mean, to be fair, he usually won them, and he wasn't picking on people smaller than him either. I mean, he was a big guy himself, six foot, pretty ripped, some tribal tattoos and stuff. But he would go out to like biker bars and challenge people to fist fights, guys way bigger than him usually, and he'd kick their asses."

"Really?" Carlisle said. "How do you know that?"

"Because he would have one of his buddies film the fights," Brunelle answered. "We got a whole bunch of video when they executed the search warrant on his house."

"That stuff wasn't admissible at the trial, was it?" Carlisle asked.

Brunelle shook his head. "No, but it was good background to have. He was a dangerous, angry dude and he wanted respect."

"So, what happened?"

"Some guy didn't respect him enough, I guess," Brunelle answered. "Plus, he'd graduated to carrying a gun around. Maybe to be a tough guy or maybe just in case he picked a fight with someone he couldn't beat up after all. Which is pretty much what happened."

Brunelle took a moment to recall the exact facts, and told them almost more to Nicole than Carlisle, mostly so she would correct him if he got anything wrong.

"He went to some bar near his house, right? Not looking for a fight, I don't think, just going out with some friends. Some guy bumped into him, or said something about his girlfriend, or something. It was never quite clear. Every witness gave a different story about what started the argument. But either way, Larson demanded an apology, the other guy told him to go fuck himself, and then they took it outside. The other guy was bigger than him, a lot bigger, but I'm not sure why that was a problem. It hadn't been before. But that night Larson had that gun on him, and I guess he wasn't sure he could win the fight after all. The other guy said something about kicking Larson's ass and started taking his coat off, and that's when Larson shot him. Two shots dead center, while the guy's arms were caught in his coat."

"That's pussy shit," Carlisle said, ever delicate in her choice of words.

"Agreed, and that's what I argued to the jury," Brunelle recalled, "although not in those exact words. Maybe that's what pissed him off so much."

"So, pretty easy case for you," Carlisle observed. "Just saying."

"Yeah," Brunelle agreed. "They argued self-defense, but you can't pick a fight with a guy, then shoot him while he's taking his coat off. The only real question was whether it was premeditated or just intentional. I argued that he formed the intent to kill while they were walking outside, so it was

premeditated, but the jury wasn't convinced. They hung on
Murder One, but came back guilty on Murder Two."

"That's why he's out now," Nicole said.

"Yeah," Brunelle agreed. "The judge gave him high end,
but even with the gun enhancement, it was only twenty years,
with two years off for good behavior and a year of credit for
time served in the county jail by the time the trial was over."

"Seventeen years," Carlisle did the math. "At least he got
high end."

Brunelle laughed, but darkly. "Yeah, because of what
happened when the jury came back with the guilty verdict."

"What happened?"

"He went nuts," Nicole remembered.

"Totally nuts," Brunelle said. "He jumped up onto the
defense table and started screaming at everyone, me, Jess, even
the jurors."

"Jess?" Carlisle asked. "Jessica Edwards from the public
defender's office? She was his lawyer? She's good."

"She is good," Brunelle agreed. "She and I started about
the same time. It was my first murder trial. I think it was her
second one. But he called her a worthless piece of shit. Told the
jurors they were all mother fuckers. Even told the judge to fuck
off and suck his dick."

"That'll get you high end," Carlisle commented.

"Definitely," Brunelle said. "The judge would have
given him more, but that was the max."

"So, what did he say to you?" Carlisle asked. "I mean, I
get that Jess was worthless and the jurors were all fuckers, but
what did he say that makes you think he wanted to kill you?"

Brunelle looked again to Nicole. "Was it when he said,
'I'm gonna fucking kill you, Brunelle'?"

Nicole nodded. "Yes, I believe it was."

"Is that all he said?" Carlisle asked. "Just, 'I'm gonna kill you'?"

"Well, first of all, that would be enough," Brunelle made sure to clarify. "But no, it was a little more specific than that."

"Yeah," Nicole agreed.

"As I recall," Brunelle continued, "he said something to the effect of: 'I'm gonna kill you, Brunelle. I'm gonna fucking murder you. I'm not gonna forget what you did to me. I'm gonna think of it every day I'm in prison, and then, when I get out, I'm still gonna be young, but you're gonna be fucking old. I'm gonna find you. I'm gonna watch you. I'm gonna know exactly what you do, and where you go, and who you're with, and I'm gonna be there. And I'm gonna fucking kill you. Slow. Just like the next fifteen years are gonna be slow for me. I'm gonna make you feel every fucking day of prison I have to do.' That's what he said."

"That's a really long threat," Carlisle noted.

"Well, like I said, he was up on the table," Brunelle explained, "and he was a big guy. It took a while until the guards could get a hold of him."

"And even then he was still shouting," Nicole said.

Brunelle nodded. "Yeah, that last bit about making it slow, that was while they were dragging him out of the courtroom."

"And now he's out," Nicole reminded everyone.

"And he's gonna murder me," Brunelle added. He tried to shake the thought from his head. "So, anyway, Gwen, you sure you don't want in on my new case?"

"Are you fucking kidding me?" Carlisle answered. "I'm not going to be standing anywhere near you until this shitstorm blows over."

CHAPTER 6

Carlisle could refuse to stand anywhere near him, but not everyone had the choice to avoid Brunelle's proximity. When Brunelle went down to court that afternoon, the judge presiding over the arraignments would be professionally obligated to be within collateral damage range. So, too, would Harris's defense attorney, whoever that turned out to be— although Brunelle had his suspicions.

One never knew, of course, but this Kevin Harris guy didn't seem to have the money to hire a private attorney. For one thing, he told Cooper one of his three motives was to get money from a single mom of two who couldn't afford a babysitter. Retainers on murder cases weren't exactly cheap, unless some young attorney lowballed the fee just to get experience. But you didn't want to be the one they got experience on. You wanted to be the one after they get all that experience. You wanted somebody who'd been defending murder cases as long as Brunelle had been prosecuting them. You wanted…

"Jessica Edwards," Brunelle greeted his oft opponent

and ever colleague as she stepped into the courtroom. "Fancy meeting you here. Again."

"Round three hundred and twelve, it seems like," Edwards replied. "You gotta stop charging my clients with murder, Dave."

"Your clients gotta stop murdering people, Jess," Brunelle returned. "You here on the Harris case, then?"

Edwards shrugged. "Yep. Kevin Harris. Any chance you're not going to charge him?"

Brunelle reached into the file he was carrying and extracted the copy of the criminal complaint marked 'DEFENSE'. He handed them to Edwards. "No chance."

Edwards accepted the documents and glanced them over quickly. "Murder One?" she questioned. "You sure you can prove premeditation?"

"Pretty sure," Brunelle answered. "He confessed."

"Hm." Edwards frowned slightly. "We'll see."

"What does that mean?"

"It means we'll see," Edwards repeated. "I don't usually agree with everything in your reports. We'll see if he really confessed, and if so, whether he confessed to premeditation."

"He punched her, and when she slapped him back, he picked up a knife," Brunelle argued. "That's enough time to form premeditation."

"That's what you say," Edwards replied evenly.

"That's what your guy said," Brunelle said.

"That's what your cop says my guy said," Edwards clarified. "And I say, we'll see."

Brunelle would have continued the argument, but the judge took the bench at that moment, and they, along with everyone else in the courtroom, were exhorted by the bailiff to

"All rise! The King County Superior Court is now in session, The Honorable Linda Stephenson presiding."

Stephenson was a good enough judge, so Brunelle wasn't worried about how the arraignment would go. He also wasn't worried because there wasn't much that could happen at the arraignment anyway; it would be hard for it to go wrong, at least for him. The only purpose of the arraignment was to advise the defendant of the charges, set an appropriate bail, and start the speedy trial clock ticking down toward the trial date. Harris already knew he was charged with murder, and now his lawyer knew what degree. The only variable was the bail amount, but Brunelle wasn't too worried about that. Public defender meant he didn't have any assets, and Murder One meant at least a million dollars bail. Harris wasn't going anywhere.

"Are there any matters ready?" Judge Stephenson asked from the bench above them.

Brunelle threw Edwards an 'Are you ready?' look. Edwards replied with an 'I'm always ready' grin and nod. Then they both stepped up to the bar.

"Good afternoon, Your Honor," Brunelle greeted the judge, then announced the case. "The parties are ready on the matter of *The State of Washington versus Kevin Harris.*"

Brunelle nodded to the guard standing by the secure door to the holding cells behind the courtroom. The guard nodded back, opened the door, and called inside for Harris. A few moments later, out walked the same man Brunelle had seen in the early hours of that morning, but wearing red jail scrubs and plastic slippers. He didn't look any less defiant though.

Harris stepped up next to Edwards and Judge Stephenson initiated the formality of the arraignment. It might have been a bumpier ride if Harris had been allowed to speak, but he had that lawyer he asked for, so she would do the talking for him.

"I have before me the complaint charging the defendant with one count of murder in the first degree," Stephenson said. "Has the defense received a copy of the charging documents?"

"Yes, Your Honor," Edwards answered. "We would waive further formal reading and enter a plea of not guilty."

"A plea of not guilty will be entered," Stephenson confirmed. She turned to Brunelle. "Conditions of release?"

"The State is asking for bail in the amount of two million dollars, Your Honor," Brunelle responded. One million was the floor, but it was a particularly brutal murder, and Harris's attitude with Chen didn't give Brunelle confidence that he would necessarily come back to court if given the chance to walk free pending trial.

Stephenson nodded and looked to the other side again. "Ms. Edwards?"

"The defense would reserve argument on the issue of bail, Your Honor," Edwards explained. "I have not received the police reports yet and would prefer to have reviewed those before making any bail argument."

Smart, in a way. Judges didn't want to hear bail arguments constantly from defendants wanting to get out of jail. It would be like having a courtroom full of kids asking, 'Are we there yet? Are we there yet?' So, there was an understanding that the defense could only argue bail one time, unless there was a substantial change of circumstances after that first argument. And 'But my client really, really wants to get out' wasn't going to cut it as a change in circumstances. Reserving argument assured Edwards would, when the time came, make the best possible argument she could for the release of her client. It also assured, in the meantime, that Brunelle would get exactly what he asked for.

"Bail will be set at two million dollars then," Judge Stephenson announced. "Anything further?"

Brunelle went through his mental arraignment checklist. Complaint filed. Formal reading waived. Not guilty plea entered. Bail set. And that speedy trial clock started automatically, so no need to address that. "No, Your Honor. I believe that's everything."

Another nod to the guard and Harris was led back into the bowels behind the bench. Brunelle looked to Edwards. "Good to see you again, Jess."

"You, too, Dave," she replied, already turning toward the exit. "Take care."

'*Take care.*' That reminded him. He needed to tell Edwards about Larson getting released. But she was already halfway out of the courtroom. And already halfway toward him was an approaching group of civilians, of mixed generations, looking sad and angry and afraid all at the same time. Brunelle knew that look. They were what the professionals called 'the victim family', and Brunelle needed to talk to them first. His warning to Edwards would have to wait.

CHAPTER 7

Brunelle hated meeting with the victim family. At least he had the script memorized.

"It's a pleasure to meet all of you," he said, gesturing toward the guest chairs crowded into his office. There weren't usually enough chairs for five people, but Nicole had grabbed a few from the offices next door. "Please, sit down."

It wasn't that Brunelle didn't like talking with people. He wasn't exactly an extrovert, but he wasn't a misanthrope either.

Amelia's family seemed nice enough. The kind of family you'd start up a conversation with if they were at the next picnic table at the park, maybe send the kids to go off and play together. Amelia's father and mother were in their sixties, divorced a long time ago, but managing to come together in this time of tragedy. Amelia's sister was in her thirties, her sadness unconcealed, her attention nevertheless divided between the topic of the meeting and keeping her two preschoolers from breaking anything in Brunelle's office. Amelia's brother was late twenties, arms crossed, obviously angry, avoiding Brunelle's eyes. Which was fine with Brunelle.

It wasn't even that the family was unlikely to provide anything of value for the case. Even if they did, Brunelle would have to direct them to the cops anyway for a formal statement that could be properly preserved and provided to the defense as required by the court rules. But that didn't mean they didn't want to help.

"Is there anything we can do to help you?"

"What do you want us to say?"

"Do you know about all the other bad things Kevin has done?"

No.

The truth.

Not relevant, not admissible.

What Brunelle hated was what the family always wanted from him. Three things, none of which he could deliver.

The first thing they wanted was a promise that the murderer would be found guilty. But juries were unpredictable—almost by design—so no matter how strong the case, Brunelle could never promise a conviction. That wasn't what the family wanted to hear, but at least it was out in the open, and dealt with easily enough.

"He's going to be convicted, right?"

"How strong is the case?"

"Promise us you're going to convict him."

There's no guarantee what a jury will do.

I can't discuss the details of the case with potential witnesses.

I can't promise that.

The second thing they wanted was punishment, and a lot of it. Brunelle could conditionally promise some punishment—conditional on that conviction he couldn't actually promise—but it was going to be less than what they wanted. A lot less.

"Can he get the death penalty?"

"He's going away for life, right?"

"He'll die in prison, right?"

Not since the State Supreme Court struck it down a few years back.

Twenty-five years, maybe thirty, max. A lot less if the jury comes back Murder Two.

Depends on when he dies.

The third thing the victim family always wanted was unspoken, and therefore the hardest to deal with. But Brunelle had been doing homicides long enough to know they all wanted it, none of them knew it, and none of them would ever get it.

There were no explicit questions for the third thing. It lived between the questions. In the glisten of Sister's eyes; in the restraint of Brother's fists; in Father holding Mother's hand for the first time in a decade. It was hope. But it was wasted.

The justice system was organized around the concept of making victims whole again. To be sure, there was also an aspect of revenge, but even that could have a healing effect on the victim. If you crash into my car, you pay for the repairs. If you steal from me, you pay for what you took. If you break my jaw, you pay my medical bills. And you go to jail, which will make me feel better, knowing you're being punished. In the end, I'll be somewhere close to where I was before you did what you did to me.

But murder was different. The unconscious expectation was the same, bleeding in from its ubiquity everywhere else in the system, but the result was impossible. It was a question they didn't even know they were asking.

'If you win, it will bring Amelia back, right?'

And it was an answer they wouldn't truly feel until even the guilty verdict didn't fill the holes in their hearts.

No. She's never coming back.

Brunelle had reached the end of the script. There were variations and some ad-libs—even a forgotten line or two, he was sure—but the conversation always made its way to the same conclusion and Brunelle always managed to steer it back to his parting line.

"Thank you for coming." He stood up from his desk and extended a hand. "As I said, I can't promise the result, but I can promise we will do everything in our power to bring what justice we can to Amelia's murderer."

And scene.

Family, exit stage left.

Brunelle, sits down at desk again.

Lights, fade to black.

CHAPTER 8

"How was your day, honey?"

Casey Emory, detective with the suburban Bellevue Police Department and girlfriend extraordinaire, greeted Brunelle in the courthouse lobby at 6:00 p.m. with a gun on her hip and a kiss on his cheek. He was glad for both.

"Same shit, different family," Brunelle offered a shrug and half a grin.

Emory cocked her head at him.

"New case," Brunelle explained. He put his arm around her shoulder, and they turned toward the exit. "I'll tell you about it over dinner."

"Ooh, dinner and a story," Emory leaned into the boyfriend's embrace. "I love hearing about your new cases. I mean, except for the dead person part. There's a dead person, right?"

Brunelle nodded. "Yes. Dead person."

"Yeah, I don't like that part," Emory repeated. "But at least we won't have to make awkward small talk while we wait for the check."

"Are dates with me that bad?' Brunelle shook his head at her.

Emory only offered a noncommittal grunt. "Hey, I agreed to meet you for dinner. I mean I was already downtown meeting with the Seattle cops about that county-wide robbery spree, but still, I could have just driven back over the bridge. So, consider yourself lucky."

"Wow, you are quite the romantic," Brunelle laughed. They stepped outside and Brunelle hesitated. "Wait, who's driving?"

"Let's take your car," Emory suggested. "I can leave mine overnight at the precinct if need be."

Brunelle managed a full grin that time, a lurid one, and an eyebrow raised in what he hoped was an alluring way, although he suspected he probably missed the mark, just a bit. "Overnight, huh?"

Emory laughed, but didn't look up to meet his lurid and alluring gaze. "Maybe. Let's see how dinner goes."

Brunelle relaxed his expression and smiled genuinely to himself. He squeezed her a little tighter and began walking again, south on Fourth Avenue.

Emory was the one who hesitated then. She glanced in the opposite direction. "Don't you park in that crappy little lot up on Sixth?"

Brunelle shook his head. "Not anymore. When I took my leave—"

"Our vacation," Emory interjected with a smile.

"Right," Brunelle agreed. "Our vacation. I lost my parking space because of our vacation. Now I have to park in that crappier little lot down on Eighth."

Emory looked all around, including at the freeway

hunching over them a few blocks to the east. "Can you even get to Eighth from here?"

"Eighth and Yesler," Brunelle expounded.

"Damn, that's a hike," Emory commented. "I guess you can start telling me about your day now."

The phrase 'your day' instead of 'your new case' sparked a memory in Brunelle's mind, and not a good one. His chest tightened a bit, and he realized he might want to talk to his boss about getting a closer parking space after all. "Yeah, actually there's another thing that happened that I probably better tell you about."

So, he told her about Jacob Larson. About that case, that verdict, that threat, and the report from Nicole that he had been released from prison. It was a long story, with a lot of clarifying questions from Emory. By the time Brunelle had finished, they had reached that crappier little parking lot at Eighth and Yesler.

"Wow," Emory breathed. "Good thing you're dating a cop."

"That does seem to keep coming up as a benefit," Brunelle acknowledged. He reached out and opened his car door. But he stopped before pulling it all the way open.

"What's wrong?' Emory asked, making her way around to the passenger side.

Brunelle frowned. "It didn't beep when I grabbed the handle. It was unlocked."

"Did you forget to lock it?"

Brunelle looked around at the crappier little parking lot. "Here? Not likely."

Emory nodded and went into cop mode. "Don't touch anything." She hovered one hand over her sidearm and came around to Brunelle's side of the car. She pushed the door all the way open with her knee. "Is anything missing?"

Brunelle peered in. "It doesn't look like it."

"There's stuff strewn all across the seats," Emory pointed out.

Brunelle shrugged. "I've been awake since one in the morning. I forgot I needed to clean it out for our dinner."

Emory stepped closer and examined the interior of the vehicle. "You know you can throw out garbage somewhere besides your back seat, right? They have trash cans now."

"Ha," Brunelle didn't laugh. "Just shove everything in the back. I'll clean it out later."

"That's what she said," Emory joked, relaxing her trigger hand.

Brunelle's eyes widened. "Wow," was all he could manage to say.

Emory laughed, but directed the subject back to the suspected vehicle prowl. "Looks like you just forgot to lock it after all, silly." She went back around to the passenger door and climbed in next to Brunelle. "I guess you were tired. Maybe I should go home early tonight."

"Not after that comment." Brunelle gave her knee a squeeze, then prepared to start the car. "You can't make a comment like that and— Shit."

"Um, gross, Dave." Emory wrinkled her nose at him. "You're not very good at this, are you?"

"No, I mean, shit, something's not right," Brunelle responded.

"What is it?"

Brunelle wasn't sure at first. The car was its usual mess, but there were certain things that he kept in certain places. One of those things was the pass card to exit the parking lot. He kept it in the coin compartment by his left knee. It wasn't in there. But his vehicle registration and insurance card were. Those were supposed to be in his glove box.

He reached across and opened the glove box, cracking it into Emory's knees.

"What's wrong, Dave?" She ignored the smack to her legs.

"Everything," he answered, opening the center console to confirm. "Everything's wrong."

"Is something missing?" Emory asked.

"No." Brunelle shook his head. "Nothing is missing. But everything is moved. Nothing is where it's supposed to be."

Emory tried a joke, jabbing a thumb at the mess in the back seat. "How can you tell?"

"I can tell," Brunelle assured her. "The pass card is in the center console instead of the coin compartment. My registration and insurance are in the coin compartment instead of the glove box. And all the shit that's usually in the center console is in the glove box."

Emory looked at the pile of fast-food napkins, receipts, and gum wrappers spilling out of the glove box. "Are you sure?"

"I'm sure."

"And you're sure nothing's missing?" Emory pressed.

"I'm sure about that too," Brunelle answered. Then he remembered one more thing and jumped out of the car. "Oh, shit."

"What?" Emory scrambled out after him, even as he was opening the trunk. "What is it?"

"My gun," Brunelle explained. He relaxed a bit when he saw the gun case still in its usual position in the trunk, wedged in the corner behind the spare tire. "Whew. It's still here."

"Is it?" Emory questioned. "Open it."

Brunelle popped open the case. "Fuck." The gun was gone.

"I'm actually a little surprised." Emory placed a hand on her chin. "I thought he'd let you keep it. Just so you'd know he isn't afraid of you."

"Who?"

"That Jacob Larson guy," Emory answered.

"Larson?" Brunelle scoffed. But he couldn't quite dismiss the suggestion, despite the strongest desire to do exactly that. "Why do you think it's him?"

"Well, it obviously wasn't a car prowler," Emory explained. "Car prowlers actually steal stuff. They don't just rearrange everything."

"He stole the gun," Brunelle pointed out.

Emory frowned. "Yeah, that's probably not good."

"But why would he do this?" Brunelle still wanted to deny the obvious truth.

"He's messing with you," Emory said. "He probably figures, correctly, you got notified when he was released. He wants you to know he hasn't forgotten about you. He wants you to know he knows where you are, and he can get to you. He wants you to know you're not safe. He wants you worried."

Brunelle frowned at his car and the empty gun case.

It worked.

CHAPTER 9

They spent that night at Emory's and not because Brunelle's story was so great at dinner. It was because his story on the way to his car was so bad. What made it even worse was that they had ruined any chance of recovering fingerprints by rummaging around the car themselves. Okay, himself, Brunelle admitted. Emory hadn't touched anything. Although they both agreed, Larson probably wore gloves anyway.

The panic of that moment began to fade over the next days as nothing more happened, and Brunelle settled back into the comfort of his usual schedule. One part of that schedule was court, especially preliminary hearings like pretrial conferences. And one of the cases scheduled for a pretrial conference was *State v. Kevin Harris*. Brunelle had noted the date well in advance. It was the opportunity to see if he and the defense attorney could work out some sort of plea bargain, which was always an important benchmark in any case because, if no deal was worked out, then trial preparation began in earnest. More importantly, at least to Brunelle right then, it was also the next time he knew for sure he would see Jessica Edwards, and he really needed to tell her about Larson.

Brunelle arrived for the pretrial right on time, which was sort of his thing. Edwards was already there, having arrived early, which was her thing.

"Hey, Jess," Brunelle greeted her. He pulled out a chair next to her at one of the several tables in the large room that the attorneys called 'The Pit'. It was there that arguments were made, deals were struck, justice was done. Or that was the theory. More often than not, neither side saw a reason to give in just yet, and cases were confirmed for the trial docket. Brunelle knew that was, by far, the likeliest outcome of their negotiations over the Harris case.

"Hey, Dave," Edwards answered. "You got an offer for me on Mr. Harris?"

It was his offer that made settlement so remote. "Sort of." He reached into his case file and extracted the formal offer sheet. The one they kept a copy of in case some less scrupulous defense attorney claimed another prosecutor had made a different, and invariably better offer. He handed the sheet to Edwards. He would have been lying if he said the fact that Larson was already out after only 17 years hadn't been weighing on his mind when he formulated the offer for Harris. On the other hand, Edwards didn't even know to ask him that. Not yet anyway.

"Plead guilty as charged, Murder One?" Edwards read the offer aloud, full scoff. "Thirty years. That's crazy."

"It's the mid-point of his range on a Murder One," Brunelle defended. "After trial, I can ask for the high end."

"Which is only three years more," Edwards pointed out. "This isn't an offer. I can get better than this at trial."

"You think so?" Brunelle challenged. But it was more of

a *pro forma* challenge. She was probably right.

"I know so," Edwards answered. "First of all, you're going to have a hell of a time proving premeditation. He didn't go over there to kill her. He went over there for something else, and things got out of control."

"Sex, drugs, and money," Brunelle specified Harris's reasons for going to Amelia's that night. "And he murdered her. That's a bit more than things just getting out of control."

"You know what I mean, Dave," Edwards responded. "This wasn't planned beforehand. Even if he did intend to kill her—"

"He stabbed her eleven times," Brunelle interjected.

Edwards offered a noncommittal roll of her shoulders. "Even if he eventually intended to kill her," she repeated, "that intent was formed in the moment. It wasn't premeditated."

"I don't need plastic sheeting and a grave already dug out back," Brunelle reminded her. "Premeditation can be formed in a split second. I just need 'more than a moment in time', and the jury is going to be instructed of that. At some point he grabbed the knife, and, in that moment, it became premeditated."

"That can't be the law, Dave, and you know it," Edwards insisted. "Otherwise, every single Murder Two would be a Murder One."

"Agree to disagree," Brunelle dismissed further argument. "In front of the jury. We will disagree in front of the jury and let them decide."

Edwards shook her head at her long-time opponent. "That's not the only problem you have with the case, Dave. I'm not sure you'll even be able to prove it was my guy who did it."

Brunelle's face screwed up into a puzzled frown, and he

cocked his head at her. "He confessed. The murder weapon was on his kitchen counter."

Edwards grinned at him. "Agree to disagree." It was far too confident of a grin for Brunelle's comfort.

"What do you mean?" he asked. "You've seen the police reports now. It's all in there."

"Oh, I've seen it," Edwards agreed. "But the jury isn't going to. It's all going to be suppressed. The confession, the murder weapon, everything you have tying him to the crime scene."

"What? Why?" Brunelle was incredulous. And curious. And just the tiniest bit worried. Edwards was a damn good lawyer, and she didn't bluff.

"Because your cop went into my guy's home without a warrant to get that confession and that murder weapon. That's an illegal entry and a violation of my client's constitutional rights. Everything obtained after that is going to be suppressed."

Brunelle took a moment to recall his conversation with Sgt. Cooper, and to remember what Cooper had written in his report. Luckily, they were the same.

"He arrested your guy outside on the porch," Brunelle said. "Just past the threshold of the front door. He doesn't need a warrant for that."

"My guy says different," Edwards replied. "He says he was inside the house, and your cops pushed their way in and grabbed him."

"Your guy is lying," Brunelle asserted.

"I don't think so," Edwards answered confidently. Again, too confidently. "I think your cop is lying."

Brunelle actually relaxed a bit at that allegation. He

wasn't a fan of defense attorneys accusing cops of lying, but it was a common enough tactic. It also never worked.

"Why do you think my cop was lying?" Brunelle asked. He could be relaxed about the allegation, but he still needed details to be able to refute it.

"Because my guy doesn't know that it matters," Edwards answered. "He doesn't know his confession and everything else would be suppressed. He was just telling me what happened. But your cop knows. That's why he lied."

Brunelle frowned. There was a logic to Edwards's argument. "So, you're saying my cop is a liar?"

"Yes," Edwards confirmed.

"And you want me to reduce the murder charge against your client who did, in fact, commit murder, because my cop is a liar?"

Edwards nodded. "Yes again."

"What am I supposed to say when the cop asks me why I cut your guy a—you want a Murder Two?"

"Manslaughter One, actually." Edwards had her counteroffer ready. "Seven years."

Brunelle couldn't stifle a chuckle at the audacity of that. "Okay, even better. So, when the cop asks me why I reduced a premeditated murder to a manslaughter, I should tell him it's because he's a liar?"

"Sure," Edwards agreed.

"Based on the word of a confessed murderer?"

"Let's say manslaughterer," Edwards suggested, "but yes."

Brunelle ran a hand over his head. "You know I can't do that, Jess."

"I do know that, Dave," Edwards answered. She pulled a

form out of her own case file and handed it to him. "That's why I've already scheduled the suppression hearing. Your cop will probably just lie again, but I'm going to make him do it on the stand."

Brunelle was so stunned by the allegation against his cops, he forgot all about Jacob Larson. But not for long.

CHAPTER 10

A few days later found Brunelle at his desk, examining Cooper's report with a fine-tooth comb, looking for any inconsistencies, either internal to his own report or with any of the other evidence in the case. If Cooper was lying, Brunelle would have to confront him about it. And you don't accuse a cop of lying without having everything lined up in advance.

It was detail work, requiring focus and concentration. So, of course, his phone rang.

Brunelle sighed, then looked at the caller I.D. It was Chen. He sighed again. He always answered when Chen called.

"Homicides. Brunelle."

"I'm homicides," Chen said. "You're the prosecutor."

"The homicide prosecutor," Brunelle defended.

"Hm," Chen grunted noncommittally. "Well, Mr. Homicides, I'm calling to see if you've got some time in your busy homicide prosecutor schedule to go on a field trip."

"A field trip?" Brunelle was intrigued. "To where?"

"Clallam Bay Corrections Center," Chen answered. "It's a four-hour drive, and I hate driving alone. Besides, I think you might be interested in what's there."

"What's there?" Brunelle asked. He was interested.

"Larson's cellmate," Chen answered, "and he wants to talk."

CHAPTER 11

The drive to Clallam Bay actually took a little over three and a half hours. Chen seemed not to like driving at all and addressed that by trying to get the trip done as quickly as possible. Easier to do when you know you can flash a badge if you get pulled over. Harder to do on the winding state highways of Washington's Olympic Peninsula. When they finally reached the prison, Brunelle was both grateful for the car to stop and already dreading the ride home.

But first, there was the little matter of a cellie turning snitch.

Clallam Bay Corrections Center was one of Washington's two maximum security prisons, the other being the more famous 'Walla Walla'—the officially named Washington State Penitentiary on the other side of the Cascade Mountains in sunny Walla Walla, Washington. The locals there wanted to be famous for their wineries, but everyone else knew 'Walla Walla' meant the prison. The worst of the worst went there. The next worse went to Clallam Bay. That included Jacob Larson. But it also included whoever this cellie-turned-snitch was.

"Michael Granzetti." Chen provided the name of the inmate to the front desk officer. "We have an appointment with Director Gordon."

They weren't called 'wardens' anymore apparently, Brunelle noted. Or maybe he and Chen didn't rate the actual warden and were getting some middle management director to chaperone their visit to Mikey the Snitch.

It took a few minutes for Director Gordon to come get them, so Chen paced the waiting room while Brunelle stared out the window at mostly just the parking lot. The waiting room was fairly full of family and friends waiting to see their incarcerated loved ones. Brunelle didn't much feel like sitting next to anyone lest they strike up a conversation with anything along the lines of, 'What brings you here today?' or 'What do you do for a living?' Better staring at rows of parked cars and cracked cement than that. Mercifully, Gordon didn't take more than those few minutes, and soon enough Brunelle and Chen were escorted inside the corrections center.

"Long drive?" Gordon made small talk as they walked deeper into the prison. He knew damn well it was a long drive from Seattle.

"This isn't the kind of thing you do over the phone," Chen replied.

"Well, I can't argue with that," Gordon laughed amiably. He was a big man, heavyset, with sandy hair and a matching, neatly trimmed beard. He was wearing a suit, not a corrections officer uniform, so Brunelle was no closer to solving the mystery of his actual position in the facility's hierarchy. "We've got Granzetti in an interrogation room waiting for you. We had to make it look like he violated rules and is being punished. Last thing any of us want is for the other prisoners to think he's a snitch. He wouldn't last the week, and the paperwork for an inmate death is, well, killer, if you'll pardon the expression."

Brunelle left it to Chen to pardon anything. He was finding himself becoming increasingly fixated on what Michael Granzetti had to say. He'd avoided thinking about it too much on the way over, able to distract himself with watching Chen almost, but not quite, drive off the miniscule shoulder of the roads. But now that they were at the prison, walking to meet Larson's cellmate, Brunelle found his stomach tightening and his ears rushing. This wasn't background on just another murder case. It was background on his own murder.

Time to make more small talk.

"Sorry for any inconvenience," Brunelle offered.

"Oh, it's no inconvenience," Gordon assured heartily. "Truth is, it's good for these guys to have something different to do. Anything to give them a little hope."

"Well, I'm not sure how much hope we can give him," Brunelle cautioned.

"You're here," Gordon pointed out. "He's already got hope. All you can do now is dash it."

Great, Brunelle frowned. *Maybe they'll both want to kill me.*

Before he could think any more morose thoughts, Gordon announced, "We're here!" and used a heavy metal key to open a heavy metal door at the terminus of the hallway they'd been travelling. Gordon held the door open, and Brunelle let Chen walk through first—just in case. No one was talking about wanting to kill Chen.

They had reached yet another white cinderblock hallway, but this one had a door on one side with two uniformed guards standing outside it. Brunelle figured Granzetti was on the other side of that door, likely accompanied by another armed guard or two. Gordon confirmed it.

"The prisoner is in that conference room." Gordon nodded to the guards, who did not nod in reply, and opened the door. "After you."

Again, Brunelle demurred to Chen. He couldn't be sure about that third armed guard. Chen almost managed not to roll his eyes, but he acquiesced and entered first, followed again by Brunelle, and finally Gordon, who pulled the door closed behind them.

The room appeared to be some sort of prisoner library. There were waist-high bookshelves against two walls, filled mostly with worn paperbacks. The third wall had a row of chairs, and seated at a small table against the fourth wall was Michael Granzetti, handcuffed, with a guard on either side, standing close enough to grab him if the need arose, but far enough away to prevent being lunged at themselves. He looked secure. And he looked different from what Brunelle had been expecting, although he wasn't exactly sure what that was.

He wasn't some lumbering hulk, 6'6" with a bald head, no neck, and tattoos from his face to his wrists. He also wasn't some sniveling worm, short and skinny, with greasy hair and shifty eyes. No, he just looked like a normal, middle-aged man. Someone you wouldn't look at twice on the street. A guy at the gym. A dad at the park. Or, apparently, a prisoner at a maximum security prison.

And it seemed Brunelle wasn't the only one playing the expectations game.

Granzetti sized up Brunelle and Chen and grinned. "You guys look just like I thought you would." He nodded toward Brunelle. "Especially you. You're the prosecutor Jake's gonna kill, right?"

"I hope not," Brunelle answered, a bit taken aback by the certainty of the prediction.

"No," Chen stepped in to assert. "He's the prosecutor we're going to stop Larson from killing. And you're the informant who's going to help us."

"Maybe." Granzetti shrugged. "Depends on what I get in return."

"Not much," Brunelle admitted. "We can't reduce your sentence, even if we wanted to."

"Which we don't," Chen added.

"What do you want?" Brunelle asked. They were still standing by the door. It had been a long drive, but they wouldn't bother sitting down if Granzetti was going to ask for the moon.

"Not much, actually," Granzetti answered. "I don't have any loyalty to Jake. He was a good cellmate, but I don't owe him anything. He talked a bit too much, but now I can cash in on that."

"Maybe you can," Brunelle cautioned. "I'll ask again: what do you want?"

"I know you can't reduce my sentence," Granzetti said, "but maybe you can change where I serve it. If I help you, I can't stay here. Snitches get stitches, right?"

"Yeah, I've heard that," Chen agreed.

"But that's fine," Granzetti went on, "because that's exactly what I want. I got four years left. My little girl just turned nine. I want to be closer to her."

"Where is she?" Brunelle asked.

"Idaho," Granzetti answered. "Near Coeur d'Alene. My ex moved back there after I went inside."

"Again," Chen reminded him. They knew Granzetti's

history.

"Again," Granzetti admitted with a grin.

"You want to transfer to an out-of-state prison?" Brunelle sighed and glanced at Gordon. He knew it could be done, but he also knew it was a lot of paperwork.

Gordon rolled his eyes a bit, but also shrugged and nodded. "It's possible. We swap prisoners sometimes. Usually when one state has too many prisoners, and the other has extra beds, not because of somebody's daughter. But," another shrug, "it can be done."

Brunelle turned back to Granzetti. "Okay. It can be done. Now make us want to do it."

Granzetti laughed a little. "Nice tough act, but we both know you're just a lawyer. That's part of why Jake hated you so much. Unjustifiably cocky, that's what he called you. And anyway, you're not fooling me. I saw how wide your eyes were when you walked in just now. You didn't drive all this way just to tell me no."

"Maybe we wanted to tell you no to your face," Chen interjected. "Then send you back into population with everyone knowing you turned snitch. Wonder how long you'd last wearing a snitch jacket."

It was Granzetti's eyes that widened, although only a bit. His lips tightened, and he was clearly trying to decide whether he had as much leverage as he thought he did.

That's when Brunelle finally felt comfortable.

People think lawyers spend all day yelling at each other. To be sure, a lot of lawyers think that's how they should practice. Movies and T.V. perpetuate that myth. So do the law schools. But the true trial lawyers, the ones who handled thousands of cases over a career and tried hundreds of them before finally hanging up their bar cards—those trial lawyers knew the key to success was identifying which cases needed to go to trial, and which ones could and should settle. Most disagreements, whether it was children fighting over the larger cookie piece, neighbors fighting over a fence line, or spouses fighting over housework, could be worked out with a mix of patience, understanding, listening, and giving enough ground to let the other side give ground, too, until you suddenly find you've met at the middle. The best lawyers weren't warriors; they were negotiators. Brunelle could battle with the best of them, but he knew how to close a deal too. Especially after a four-hour drive. He finally pulled over a chair and sat down opposite Michael Granzetti.

"Listen, Michael," he started. "Is it Michael or Mike?"

Granzetti hesitated at the sudden shift in dynamics. "Mike."

"Mike." Brunelle repeated. "Good. Okay, Mike, listen. You're right. We didn't drive all the way here just to tell you no. But you didn't ask for this meeting just not to say anything to us. What you're asking for, it's not crazy. Looks like it's something that can be done, and if you go ahead and do what you were planning on doing anyway, then we can get started on that. I bet there's an empty bed at that prison near your daughter. And I bet I'm going to be very appreciative of any information you have that might keep me from getting murdered. So, why don't we both just calm down and do what we both came here to do? You tell me whatever it is that you have to tell me, and then we can start filling out the paperwork to get you to Idaho. It only makes sense, right?"

Granzetti's expression froze for a moment, then softened. "I don't have all that much to offer, actually," he admitted.

"You're not asking for all that much in return, actually," Brunelle assured him. "Tell us what you know."

Chen remained standing behind Brunelle, which was probably the right call. Brunelle had Granzetti ready to talk, but he might freeze up if the cop stepped in again.

"Jake really hates you, man," Granzetti started. "Like, I've never seen anyone so fixated on getting revenge against someone. Well, I mean, someone who wasn't an ex-girlfriend or something."

"Of course," Brunelle encouraged, ignoring the larger problems of that statement.

"But he wouldn't stop talking about it," Granzetti continued. "It wasn't every day, but it was almost every day. It wasn't like he was saying he didn't do it. He just seemed to think he should have gotten away with it. Like it was no big deal, or the other guy deserved it, or something. I don't know, he probably did, right?"

Brunelle shrugged. "Maybe."

"Yeah, I thought so." Granzetti nodded. "So, like, that was why Jake was so pissed, I guess. And he totally blamed you, man. Not the jury, not the judge, not even his own lawyer. You. Because he knew you could have dismissed it at any time. But you didn't."

"No, I didn't," Brunelle agreed. "That wouldn't have been the right thing to do."

"Yeah, he said you were super self-righteous too," Granzetti almost laughed. "Always standing up in your fancy suit and talking to the judge without even looking at him or his lawyer."

"That's how you're supposed to talk in court," Brunelle instinctively defended. "You never address the other side directly."

Granzetti shrugged. "Whatever. I don't care about that shit, and Jake didn't either. He just thought you were a self-righteous prick and he was in prison because of you."

"That all sounds accurate," Chen finally jumped in again. "Now tell us what he has planned."

Granzetti looked up at the detective and frowned. "You mean, like, details?"

"Details would be good," Chen confirmed in a low growl.

"Well, see, um, I don't know the details exactly," Granzetti squirmed. "Jake was angry, but he wasn't stupid. Well, not that stupid anyway. He didn't spell it all out for me. Nothing like, first I'm gonna do this, then I'm gonna do that." Granzetti transferred his gaze back to Brunelle. "I just remember he said he was gonna take your life away the same way you took his away."

"What does that mean?" Brunelle asked.

"I'm not sure," Granzetti admitted. "But I remember the night before he got out, he said, 'Tomorrow's the day. I've been waiting seventeen years to take that fucking prosecutor's life away, and tomorrow I finally get out of here so I can do it.'"

Granzetti took a beat, then nodded again toward Brunelle. "That's you. You're the fucking prosecutor."

"I got that." Brunelle grimaced. "Thanks."

"So, no details on how he plans to do it?" Chen confirmed. "Nothing more than he's got some plan, and he's going to do it?"

"That's not nothing," Granzetti defended. "At least now you know he's serious about it."

Brunelle recalled his prowled car. "I already knew that."

Granzetti's brow furrowed. "Really?"

"Really," Brunelle answered. "But you're in luck."

"How's that?' Granzetti offered a hopeful expression.

"What you gave wasn't much," Brunelle explained, "but you're not asking for much either. I don't mind knowing for sure Larson plans to try to kill me, and I don't give a shit about where you serve the rest of your sentence."

Brunelle looked over his shoulder at Chen. "Do you care?"

Chen shrugged and looked away. "I don't care."

Brunelle glanced over at Gordon. "Can it be done?"

Gordon hesitated, but nodded. "It can be done."

Brunelle nodded, then turned back to Granzetti. "One more thing."

Granzetti's brow furrowed again. "What?"

"Did he talk about wanting to hurt anyone else?" Brunelle asked. "The judge, the cops, his own lawyer?"

Granzetti frowned and shook his head. "Nah, just you. I mean, he hated his lawyer, I can tell you that. He complained about her almost as much as you. But he never talked about killing her. It was more like, he was pissed she didn't really care about him, so he wasn't gonna care about her."

"I didn't care about him either," Brunelle said. "Not really. It was just another case."

Granzetti nodded. "Yeah, I get that. I'm doing eight years for armed robbery, but it's not like I didn't do it. We all got jobs to do, even prosecutors. But Jake? Well, I guess he didn't see it like that."

"Lucky me," Brunelle quipped.

Granzetti frowned again. "Doesn't sound lucky to me."

"It's not," Chen put in. "Are we done here?"

Brunelle thought for a moment, then stood up. "We're done."

"So, I'm gonna get transferred to Idaho?" Granzetti asked hopefully.

Brunelle shrugged. "Like I said, I don't care. I'll leave it in Director Gordon's hands. But I think you'll be okay. It's probably less paperwork than if he doesn't transfer you and you get shanked in the yard."

Brunelle and Chen took their leave, even as Gordon got hung up with an insistent and increasingly frantic Michael Granzetti.

Outside the conference room, Chen offered a half-smile. "Well, at least you know Larson hated his own lawyer too."

"Yeah, that's not too surprising," Brunelle replied.

"Really? I would think they'd like defense attorneys."

"Nobody likes defense attorneys," Brunelle opined. "Not defendants, not juries, and," he slapped Chen across the chest, "and especially not cops."

"Why especially cops?" Chen asked with a frown.

"Because," Brunelle answered, his thoughts already moving to his next task, "they're the ones who hold you guys accountable."

CHAPTER 12

A motion to suppress evidence was actually a pretty stunning concept, if one took a moment to truly consider it. It assumed the existence of evidence—actual evidence of an actual crime that someone actually committed—then asked the judge to ignore that evidence, to hide it from the jury and pretend it never existed. That took some balls.

Or rather, it didn't. Not only did Jessica Edwards not, to the best of Brunelle's knowledge and belief, have any such organs, but balls were hardly the organ to invoke for something that took toughness and courage. In fact, Brunelle couldn't think of any body part less tough or more sensitive. It was literally the universally known weak spot on the male body. It didn't take balls to bring a motion to suppress the confession and the weapon from a murder trial; it took ovaries. It took guts.

Jessica Edwards had guts. And more importantly, as they'd discussed with Michael Granzetti, she had a job to do.

"Good morning, Dave," she greeted her opponent as she approached him at the front of the courtroom a few afternoons after Brunelle's trip to Clallam Bay. They weren't in the criminal presiding court anymore. A motion like this was going to take hours, so it had been assigned out to another judge, to be heard in that judge's courtroom, with no other matters on the docket. Compared to the chaos of criminal presiding, Judge Parker's courtroom almost felt abandoned. Edwards's briefcase made an echo when she set it on the defense table and snapped open the latches.

They were both early and were the only two in the courtroom. Soon enough, though, the guards would bring in Edwards's client, Brunelle's cops would take their seats out in the hallway, and the court reporter and bailiff would appear to presage the judge emerging from her chambers and ascending to the bench.

"You ready?" Edwards asked.

"Ready to win, you mean?" Brunelle replied. "Yeah, I'm ready for that.

Edwards shook her head. "You prosecutors are always so confident. It would be cute if it weren't also so maddening."

"We both know you can't win this motion," Brunelle said.

"I can," Edwards raised an eyebrow, "if your cop tells the truth."

Brunelle considered fully engaging the argument then and there before the judge came out, but decided to keep his powder dry. "I guess we'll just have to wait and see what he does."

"I'm pretty sure I know what your cop is going to do," Edwards replied. "What I'm really interested in is, what are you going to do when he does it?"

The statement stunned Brunelle just a bit, and was followed by the further distraction of all of those aforementioned people spilling into the courtroom at once, guards and the defendant and court staff and witnesses. It was the witnesses who were the most distracting because when they walked into the courtroom, they called out, "Psst!" and gestured for him to come over. Brunelle took a moment to regain himself, then stifled a sigh and trudged past the empty gallery seats to the waiting police officers.

"Brunelle!" Sgt. Cooper clapped him a bit too roughly on the shoulder. "There he is. Good man. So, are we really going to have to go through with this? You couldn't talk the lady lawyer out of it?"

Brunelle had to take another moment to keep himself from engaging in an extra argument he didn't have time for right then. "Ms. Edwards," he replied, "has the right to note this motion. We have the right to win it. So, let's just do that as efficiently as we can. Are you both ready?"

'Both' referred to Cooper, the veteran patrol sergeant, and Jeremy Jensen, the junior officer who had been fortunate enough to accompany Cooper when they contacted and ultimately arrested Harris. Cooper was obviously ready. Brunelle was more concerned about Jensen.

But the junior officer stood up straight and offered a sharp nod. "Yes, sir. I'm ready."

Brunelle didn't always appreciate that sort of formality— they were cops, not soldiers—but he thought it would likely help him win the hearing. Cooper might well come off as a cynical old cop who would cut corners to catch the bad guys, but Jensen was just some young officer trying to do the right thing. Brunelle was glad he'd subpoenaed both of them for the hearing.

"All rise!" called out the bailiff. "The King County

Superior Court is now in session, The Honorable Samantha Parker presiding."

"Wait in the hallway," Brunelle instructed his officers. "I'll come get you one at a time."

Then he turned his back on them and hurried to the prosecution table before Judge Parker took her seat above the proceedings.

"Are the parties ready on the matter of *The State of Washington versus Kevin Harris*?" the judge asked as she took the bench.

"The State is ready," Brunelle confirmed.

"The defense is ready as well," Edwards added. "This is our motion."

"It is," Judge Parker agreed. She was at that stage in her legal career when lawyers start to become judges, somewhere in her late forties to early fifties. The ambitious ones were in their forties; the more casual ones were in their fifties. Although Parker was in those fifties now, she had been a judge for almost ten years. She was definitely ambitious. The talk around the courthouse was that she was eyeing a spot on the Court of Appeals. Right then, though, she was eyeing Jessica Edwards. "I've read your briefing. I'm interested to see how the hearing goes."

That was judge-talk for, 'We both know you're going to lose.' But Edwards simply smiled up at the judge and replied, "As am I." Defense attorney talk for, 'Fuck you.'

Judge Parker turned to Brunelle. "It's the defense's motion," she repeated, "but once the claim of a constitutional violation is asserted, the burden is on the State to prove the lawfulness of the conduct. You may call your first witness, Mr. Brunelle."

"Thank you, Your Honor." Brunelle bowed his head slightly. "The State calls Sergeant Jeff Cooper."

Might as well start with the biggest variable. If Cooper did take the stand and confirm Harris's version of events, there wouldn't be any need to call Jensen after all. And if instead, as Brunelle expected, Cooper confirmed his own version of events from his written report, well, then Jensen would still be a pretty quick witness, just tying the bow on Cooper's package, so to speak.

The announcement of Sgt. Cooper was all duly dramatic, but the drama was lost when Brunelle had to then turn around, trudge to the back of the courtroom, and open the door to the hallway to tell Cooper to come inside. By the time Cooper had entered, walked to the front, raised his right hand, and taken the witness stand, the courtroom felt less theatrical and more like the everyday, workaday place it actually was. If there had been a jury present, Brunelle would have made a conscious effort to breathe some of that drama back into the confines of the room. As it was, he just wanted to get through his direct examination as quickly as possible so Cooper could go ahead and say what he was supposed to say, and Brunelle could go ahead and win what he was supposed to win.

"Could you please state your name and occupation for the record?" Brunelle began his questioning.

Cooper looked up and delivered his answer to the judge. He knew who his audience was. "Jeff Cooper. I'm a sergeant with the Seattle Police Department."

Again, if there had been a jury, Brunelle would have gone through Cooper's resume. Years as a cop, years as a sergeant, assignments, trainings, commendations, awards, etc. But it was only a judge, and an experienced one at that. Judge

Parker had the same wrinkles around her eyes that Cooper did. They'd both been doing this a long time. She knew he was a veteran cop, and Brunelle—who had his own increasing collection of wrinkles—knew to move on.

"Were you involved in the investigation of the murder of Amelia Carter?"

Cooper gave a half-shrug and a half-nod. "I'm not sure if I was involved in the investigation of it, exactly. I'm not a detective. But I was definitely involved in arresting her murderer."

And in case anyone wasn't sure who that murderer was, Cooper punctuated his sentence by pointing across the courtroom at Harris.

"That would be the defendant, Kevin Harris?" Brunelle had to ask to make the record. Court reporters didn't take down witnesses' gestures, only their words.

Cooper nodded. "Oh yes. That's him."

Brunelle may have dispensed with the theatrics, but Cooper had brought his own. Just as well. There was nothing wrong with being a little entertained while one sought truth and justice. It would also help keep Parker's focus. Those courtrooms could get a bit stuffy, especially in the afternoons. A boring witness was an excellent sleep aid right after lunch.

"Could you please explain to the Court how you became involved in the identification, location, and arrest of Mr. Harris?"

Cooper nodded and looked up at the judge again. "I heard the callout for a possible homicide. I'm a sergeant and it was my sector, so I responded, even though I knew the detectives would be on their way too. When I arrived, there were already two patrol officers there. I tasked them to setting up a perimeter and then went up to the apartment and contacted the reporting party. She was pretty much hysterical, so not much help, but I managed to get the name of the victim out of her. I ran the victim's name, and it came back that she had been a petitioner for a protection order two years ago. The respondent in that petition was named Kevin Harris. I ran him and saw he had a bunch of domestic violence charges, just misdemeanor assault and order violations, but still. I pulled up his last known address from the Department of Licensing and headed back down to the parking lot. By then, Officer Jensen had arrived, too, so I told him to follow me in his patrol car, and the two of us went to Harris's place. It was only about a mile away, so we got there pretty quick. Jensen took up a position at the bottom of the stairs and—"

"Okay, let me interrupt you right there," Brunelle interjected. Cooper was on a roll, and Edwards hadn't objected to the blatantly narrative answer, but Brunelle wanted to go through the next bit a little more carefully. How Cooper figured out who the suspect was and where he lived was interesting, but ultimately irrelevant for the motion. What mattered was what happened when they got there.

"Can you describe the residence for us?" Brunelle asked. "Was it an apartment, a house, what?"

"It was a small house," Cooper explained. "Kind of jammed in next to a bunch of other small houses. I think they used to be for workers back in the day when everyone in Seattle was either a fisherman or a lumberjack. Anyway, that whole neighborhood now is just a bunch of rundown rentals. We get all kinds of callouts from there, let me tell you, so I wasn't surprised when Harris's address came back to there."

"Anyway, back to the house," Brunelle redirected him.

"How did you approach it?"

"Um, pretty much just head-on," Cooper seemed pleased to say. "Jensen took up a cover position at the bottom of the stairs, and I went right up to the front door and knocked."

"Okay, but before we get to that," Brunelle knew the architecture was going to be important, "was there like a porch or a front stoop or anything? Or just stairs right up to the door?"

Cooper seemed to understand the import of the question. "There was a small, covered porch. The steps led up to that, then it was about three more feet to the front door. That's where I was standing when I knocked on the door."

"Did you stand right in front of the door?" Brunelle was a little surprised by that.

"Yeah," Cooper confirmed. "Why not?"

"What if he shot through the door or something?" Brunelle posited.

Cooper took a moment, then shook his head at Brunelle. "He didn't shoot her, counselor. He stabbed her."

Brunelle thought about pointing out that Harris could have had a knife *and* a gun, but decided to move on. That kind of simplemindedness could actually bolster a person's credibility.

"Sure," he acknowledged Cooper's response without actually commenting on it. "So, okay, anyway, you knocked on the door. Did you announce yourself as 'police'?"

Another incredulous look from Cooper. "Why would I do that?"

Brunelle ignored the question and pushed ahead. "Okay, so, you knocked on the door, didn't announce yourself as police. Then what happened?"

Cooper shrugged and looked up again to Judge Parker.

"He opened the door."

Okay, Brunelle thought. *Now for the hard part.*

He didn't want to be accused of leading the witness, so he fell back on the prosecutor's favorite crutch question: "What happened next?"

"I identified myself," Cooper answered. "I was in full uniform, so he already knew I was a cop. I asked him to step outside. When he did, I detained him on suspicion of murder."

Brunelle frowned slightly. The stepping outside part was good, but the immediately into handcuffs could be its own problem.

"What was the basis for the detention?" Brunelle asked. Then, stating the applicable legal standard, in part for the record, in part for the judge, but mostly to prompt Cooper, he expanded the phrasing of the question: "What was the factual basis for your reasonable suspicion that detention of the defendant was warranted for further investigation?"

"Um, well," Cooper rubbed the back of his neck, "he was the ex-boyfriend of the victim; he had a history of domestic violence; he lived in close proximity to the crime scene; and he was awake and dressed at one o'clock in the morning."

Brunelle nodded along to each of the facts Cooper listed. Upon recitation, it felt pretty thin. Enough to talk with him. Maybe not enough to handcuff him first. Cooper must have seen Brunelle's worried expression.

"And I could see a bloody knife on the kitchen counter."

"Ah," Brunelle pointed at him. That would do it. "So, you could see the knife from where you were standing on the, uh—"

"Outside on the porch," Cooper made sure to confirm. "Yes. I mean, it was far away, and maybe you wouldn't know what you were looking at if you didn't know his ex-girlfriend had just been stabbed to death. But I knew what I was looking for, and I saw it."

Brunelle relaxed again. He was going to win the motion. Cooper said they were outside the house, and he provided sufficient facts to legally justify handcuffing Harris. There was just one more thing he had to confirm.

"Prior to speaking with the defendant, did you advise him of his constitutional rights?"

"Of course," Cooper huffed. "I'm not some rookie. I'm not going to question a murder suspect without reading him his rights."

Brunelle nodded again. "Good to hear. Did the defendant express any confusion regarding his rights?"

"No, he did not."

"Did he agree to speak with you?"

"Yes, he did."

"And what did he say?"

"He admitted to the murder," Cooper answered, if a bit conclusory.

"Can you be a little more detailed?" Brunelle encouraged.

Cooper shrugged and nodded. "Sure. He said he went over to her apartment because they used to date, and he was looking to maybe hook up with her, maybe get some money, maybe score some drugs. But she wasn't interested in any of those things and told him to leave. He wouldn't leave, so it got physical, and it escalated. Eventually he grabbed a knife from her kitchen and stabbed her. Then he fled."

"And he took the knife with him?"

"I guess so," Cooper said. "We found it at his home.

Maybe he was worried about fingerprints, I don't know. I don't really care either. We recovered the knife, and he confessed to the murder. It was a good night."

Brunelle cringed. *Not for Amelia Carter.* He'd have to tell Cooper not to use that phrase in front of the jury.

"Did he give you permission to go in and recover the knife?"

"Yes, he did."

With better facts, Brunelle would have asked Cooper if he'd also advised Harris of his right to refuse, limit, or terminate the search of his residence. But Cooper didn't do any of that, so Brunelle decided he'd play defense on that issue, if Edwards raised it. There was just one more thing to establish before he sat down.

"And Officer Jensen observed everything you just testified to, is that correct?"

"His job was to cover my ass," Cooper laughed. "He better have been watching."

Crass, but credible. "Thank you, Sergeant Cooper," Brunelle concluded. "No further questions."

Cooper came across as cynical and self-important, but that was pretty standard for a twenty-five-year beat cop. The important thing was, he didn't come across as a liar. At least not on direct examination. Cross-exam might be a different story.

"Good afternoon, Sergeant Cooper," Edwards began as she stalked up to the witness stand. Brunelle sat down to watch the show. He hoped it fell short of the early reviews.

"Good afternoon, counselor," Cooper returned, pleasantly enough, but his body language had changed noticeably. With Brunelle, he'd been relaxed and confident, almost slouching as he fielded the prosecutor's questions. With

Edwards, he was bolt upright, leaning forward slightly. It was an aggressive posture. Brunelle almost expected him to hover a hand over his hip holster.

"I'd like to get right to the crux of the matter," Edwards said. "I'm not interested—today at least—in how you located my client. I want to talk about exactly what happened when you contacted him at his residence. In fact, you just testified that you knew it was his residence, correct?"

"It was his last known address, according to his driving record," Cooper answered. He was already fighting with her, even over the difference between 'address' and 'residence'. Brunelle frowned.

"And he lived there, right?" Edwards pressed.

"He was there that night," Cooper continued to resist Edwards's characterization. "That's all I cared about."

Edwards took a moment, gears turning, then asked, "Do you think he would have had a different Fourth Amendment interest against search and seizure if he was at a location other than his personal residence?"

An interesting question. But a legal one. "Objection," Brunelle stood up. "That calls for a legal conclusion, and a nuanced one at that. This witness is here to recount facts. Your Honor will make the necessary legal conclusions."

Judge Parker nodded. "Sustained. Save this for your argument, counsel," she instructed Edwards.

Edwards wasn't fazed. She had maybe stumbled on an additional issue to argue at the conclusion of the hearing. Brunelle wondered how many more Cooper might hand her.

"So, you knocked on his door?" Edwards asked. "This armed murder suspect? Weren't you afraid?"

"Afraid?" Cooper rejected the very notion. "I've been

doing this a long time, ma'am. I'm not afraid of doing my job."

"So, none of the so-called 'officer safety concerns' we always hear about?" Edwards prodded.

"Officer safety concerns are always a priority, ma'am," Cooper returned. "But being safe isn't the same thing as being afraid."

"Plus, you had Officer Jensen covering your," Edwards paused at the choice of her next word, "position. Is that correct?"

"Correct," Cooper confirmed. "If your client had tried anything, Officer Jensen would have taken him out."

Edwards nodded. "Okay. Well, good to know, I suppose. So, you knocked, and he just opened the door? This man who had allegedly just murdered someone in cold blood simply opened the door for a uniformed police officer? Oh, and he left the alleged murder weapon where you could see it? Is that all correct, Sergeant?"

"I'm not sure it was in cold blood, counselor," Cooper said. "I think he was pretty upset. You'd think that, too, if you saw how bloody the scene was."

"I saw the photographs," Edwards responded. "You guys never call out defense attorneys to help process the scene."

"No, ma'am," Cooper agreed. "The job is hard enough without defense attorneys second-guessing us all the time."

"Well, that's my job, I'm afraid," Edwards said, "and it's hard enough, too. So, let's do a little more of it, shall we?"

Cooper shrugged. "That's what I'm here for, counselor."

Edwards grinned at him. "It certainly is. Now, my client opened the door to his residence. This murder suspect. Murder weapon in plain view. Blood still wet. And you just politely asked him to step outside?"

Cooper nodded. "Yes, ma'am."

"Did you order him outside?" Edwards suggested.

"No, ma'am," Cooper answered. "I asked him, and he agreed."

"What did you say exactly?"

"I can't recall my exact words that night," Cooper cautioned, "but what I usually say is something like, 'Would you please step outside, sir?'"

"Usually?" Edwards questioned. "You've been in this situation before?"

"Maybe not this exact situation, ma'am," Cooper explained, "but very similar situations. I've been doing this a long time. I've arrested a lot of different people for a lot of different crimes. There's a rhythm to it. I know what I usually do, and I know I did that here. I'm not going inside without a warrant."

"But isn't that exactly what you did here?" Edwards tried to pounce. "You went inside my client's residence without a warrant to get the knife."

"He gave me permission for that, ma'am," Cooper corrected himself. "I don't need a warrant if I have permission."

That was true, Brunelle knew. So did Edwards. And Judge Parker.

Edwards frowned. Cooper wasn't the only one with a decade or two of experience. Cooper had testified the way Brunelle had expected. Edwards might have been hoping for something different, but it was clearly not going to happen.

"So, it's your testimony that you requested Mr. Harris to exit his residence, and he complied with that request?" she asked.

"That is correct, counselor."

"So, you did not reach into his home, grab him in the doorway, and pull him out of his home to handcuff him on the porch?"

Cooper locked eyes with Edwards. "No."

"Say it back to me," Edwards instructed. "I want to hear you say it specifically. Say, 'I didn't reach into his home. I didn't grab him in the doorway. I didn't pull him out onto the porch.'"

Brunelle stood up again. "Objection, Your Honor. The witness has already answered the question."

"Sustained," Judge Parker ruled. "He doesn't have to repeat after you, Ms. Edwards. He answered your question."

Edwards nodded up to the judge, then sneered at Cooper. "He certainly did." She turned her back on him. "No further questions."

Brunelle exhaled audibly.

"Any redirect examination, Mr. Brunelle?" Judge Parker asked.

No way. Redirect allowed for recross. But if Brunelle didn't ask any more questions, Edwards couldn't either. "No, Your Honor. This witness can be excused."

Judge Parker nodded. "You're excused, Sergeant Cooper," she informed him. She looked again to Brunelle. "Any further witnesses?"

"Yes, Your Honor," Brunelle answered even as Cooper was stepping down from the witness stand. "The State calls Jeremy Jensen."

"I'll grab him for you," Cooper offered as he walked past. A bit informal, but Brunelle appreciated not having to walk the length of the courtroom and back again. A few moments later, Cooper exited and a moment after that Jensen entered.

If Cooper was the grizzled old veteran, Jensen was the wide-eyed rookie. In truth, he had a few years of experience already, but he was definitely a different generation of cop from Cooper. He was tall, fit, with a crew cut so close that most of it was just skin. He marched to the front of the courtroom, stood at attention when Parker swore him in, then sat on the witness stand and stared directly at Brunelle as he began his examination.

It was going to be quick. Brunelle started with the usual 'name, rank, and serial number,' then got right to the scene at the house.

"What was your role when you arrived at the defendant's residence?"

"Sergeant Cooper instructed me to take up a position at the bottom of the stairs and cover him as he attempted suspect contact." Jensen's body language was definitely tenser than Cooper's, but that seemed consistent with his entire demeanor.

"Did you do that?"

"Yes, sir."

"So, you were able to observe the entire interaction between Sergeant Cooper and the defendant?"

Jensen hesitated. "Some of the interaction was blocked by Sergeant Cooper's body, sir."

That made sense, Brunelle supposed. "Okay, but you were watching the interaction to the best of your ability, right? In case you needed to do something to protect Sergeant Cooper?"

"That was my focus, sir," Jensen answered. "Protecting Sergeant Cooper."

Brunelle nodded. If Cooper had been too relaxed, Jensen was making up for it by being too uptight. Best to just get through the necessary testimony as quickly as possible.

"So, did you see Sergeant Cooper knock on the door?"

"Yes, sir. I saw that."

"Did you see the defendant open the door?"

"Yes, sir. I saw that."

"Did you hear Sergeant Cooper ask the defendant to step outside?"

Jensen took a moment to answer. "I was too far away to hear exactly what was said, sir."

"Okay," Brunelle said. "Did you see Sergeant Cooper ever grab the defendant while he was still in the doorway of his home?"

Another hesitation by Jensen. Brunelle would need to talk to him about that. The judge would understand he was just trying to be careful and accurate in his answers, but a jury might find it suspicious. "As I said, sir, some of my view was blocked by Sergeant Cooper's body."

Brunelle raised an eyebrow at that response. Jensen added, "But I don't recall seeing anything like that, sir."

"Do you think you would have seen it," Brunelle felt the need to follow up, "if it had happened?"

Jensen thought for a moment. "Yes, sir."

"And you didn't see it?"

"No, sir."

Brunelle exhaled. He didn't really like the vibe he was getting from Jensen. A lot of the younger cops weren't very good witnesses yet. Like anything, it took time and practice to get good at it. Cooper had delivered his answers to the judge, but Jensen was staring at Brunelle the entire time. Or rather at some spot on the wall just over Brunelle's shoulder. In any event, not the judge. Maybe Brunelle could talk to him before the trial, give him some pointers.

Brunelle took a moment to assess whether to ask any more questions. He could ask Jensen to recount what Harris had said about the murder, but Cooper had already put that into the record. Jensen's job was just to corroborate the steps Cooper had taken during the contact and arrest. He had done that. "Thank you, officer. No further questions."

Brunelle sat down and Edwards stood up. Jensen's head swiveled toward her as she approached him. Brunelle might have expected Jensen to get even more tense as Edwards approached, but he wasn't sure that was even possible.

"How long have you been a police officer, Officer Jensen?" she began.

"Three years in August, ma'am."

"How long do you want to be a police officer, Officer Jensen?"

Jensen cocked his head at her. "Um, my entire career, ma'am."

"Longer than just today?" Edwards followed up. "Longer than just this case?"

Jensen nodded slowly. "Yes, ma'am."

Edwards nodded back at him. "Is there any part of your testimony you want to change? I'm giving you that chance right now."

Jensen frowned. "No, ma'am."

"Are you sure?"

"Yes, ma'am."

Edwards frowned too, but for different, albeit related, reasons. "Well, then, no further questions."

"Any further witnesses?" Judge Parker asked Brunelle again.

He stood up. "No, Your Honor. The State rests."

The next issue was whether Harris himself would testify. With the evidence as it stood right then, Brunelle would win. Cooper said Harris stepped outside voluntarily, and Jensen backed that version up as best he could. Without Harris taking the stand and saying something to the contrary, the judge would have no choice but to rule in Brunelle's favor and deny the motion to suppress. But there were other considerations.

"All right then," Judge Parker reached for her copy of the court rules. "Now, before we go any further and I inquire of the defense whether they intend to call any witnesses, I am required to read the admonition from Criminal Rule 3.5(b) to the defendant. Mr. Harris, could I please have your attention?"

Harris looked up at the judge, but didn't say anything. He should have done that with Cooper to begin with.

"Criminal Rule 3.5, Confession Procedure, Subsection (b). 'It shall be the duty of the court to inform the defendant that: (1) he may, but need not, testify at the hearing on the circumstances surrounding the statement; (2) if he does testify at the hearing, he will be subject to cross-examination with respect to the circumstances surrounding the statement and with respect to his credibility; (3) if he does testify at the hearing, he does not by so testifying waive his right to remain silent during the trial; and (4) if he does testify at the hearing, neither this fact nor his testimony at the hearing shall be mentioned to the jury unless he testifies concerning the statement at trial.'"

In other words: you don't have to testify, and if you do testify, that doesn't mean you have to testify at the trial, but whatever you say now, you're stuck with it.

So, Edwards had a decision to make. But the decision wasn't really all that difficult. Harris could take the stand and say whatever he wanted. The judge wasn't going to believe him over two cops.

"Ms. Edwards," Judge Parker asked, "does your client wish to testify?"

Edwards stood up and gave the answer they all knew she would. "No, Your Honor. The defense rests."

And that was that. Brunelle was right. There was no way he was going to lose the hearing.

"Argument?" Judge Parker invited.

"The defense would waive argument," Edwards responded. "We concede that, based on the testimony presented today, the motion to suppress will be denied."

Judge Parker nodded and looked to Brunelle. "Would you like to argue anyway, Mr. Brunelle?"

"Lawyers do like to hear the sound of their own voices," Brunelle replied, "but I won't waste the Court's time. We would ask you to deny the motion and confirm the case for trial."

"All right then," Judge Parker said again. "I agree with Ms. Edwards's assessment that, based on the testimony presented here today, the Court has no choice but to find that the detention and arrest of the defendant was lawful, the defendant's statements were made after proper advisement and waiver of his constitutional rights, and the knife alleged by the State to be the murder weapon was collected with the consent of the defendant, which obviated the need for a warrant. The motion to suppress is denied."

The court emptied out after that, much like it had filled in. The judge left the bench, followed by her staff. The guards handcuffed Harris again and led him out a secure side door. Brunelle would have ducked into the hallway to tell the cops the good news, but they never stuck around after they testified anyway. Shortly, it was just Brunelle and Edwards again, carrying their files toward the exit.

"I told you I'd win, Jess," Brunelle teased.

"I know, Dave." Edwards shook her head at him. "But that doesn't mean you should have."

CHAPTER 13

Victories could feel short-lived in prosecution. Usually, that was because no matter how many bad guys got put away, there was always another one ready to take his place. It wasn't usually because the victory was undone before the bad guy could actually get put away.

"Mr. Brunelle, sir?"

The callout of his name coincided with a sharp knock on his office door. Brunelle looked up to see Officer First Class Jeremy Jensen standing at attention in his doorframe. He was pretty sure he knew what that meant. *Fuck.*

"Officer Jensen," he said. "What can I do for you?"

As if he didn't know.

"I need to talk with you, sir," Jensen answered.

Brunelle nodded. "I wish I weren't surprised." He gestured toward his guest chairs. "Have a seat."

Jensen straightened up a bit, which was impressive given how impossibly erect his posture already was. "I'd rather stand, sir. I feel like I should stand."

Brunelle sighed. He gestured again to the chairs. "You

should sit."

Jensen hesitated, then finally relaxed his posture the smallest amount and hurried into one of the chairs. He still looked like he was at attention.

"If it makes it any easier," Brunelle offered, "I think I know what you're going to say."

"You do?" Jensen seemed genuinely surprised. "How?"

"I've been doing this a long time," Brunelle explained. "You make friends. Friends on both sides. Friends who tell you the truth. But sometimes that isn't enough. Sometimes you need someone else to tell the truth. I think you're here to tell me the truth. Am I wrong?"

"No, sir. You're not wrong." Jensen seemed to find some small relief in Brunelle taking the lead. But then he frowned. "Does it really matter if he was inside or outside his front door?"

"Let me worry about that," Brunelle took the burden from him. "Just tell me the truth."

Jensen took a deep breath, then let out a cleansing sigh. "Sergeant Cooper didn't stand there and ask the suspect to exit the residence. He knocked, then stepped to the side so he was out of sight. When the suspect opened the door a crack, Sergeant Cooper kicked the door all the way open and grabbed the suspect by the arm. He yanked him out onto the porch, took him to the floor, and handcuffed him."

Brunelle just nodded. At least it was nice to know he could still trust Edwards to tell him the truth.

"Sergeant Cooper did read him his rights, though," Jensen added quickly, "and he did give us permission to go inside and get the knife. That matters, right?"

It didn't matter at all. But Brunelle forced a smile. "The

only thing that matters is the truth."

CHAPTER 14

"Sergeant Cooper?"

Brunelle knocked on the cubicle wall where Sgt. Cooper's workstation was, one of several dozen in a maze on one of the lower levels of Seattle P.D. headquarters. This wasn't a phone call conversation. It definitely wasn't an email.

Cooper was seated at his desk, eating lunch—a submarine sandwich that was almost but not quite falling apart in his hands. He looked up at Brunelle and swallowed his current bite. "Hey there, counselor. I'd offer you a seat, but they didn't give us enough room for extra chairs. This is just a place to stop by and check email before I head out on the street."

"That's fine," Brunelle replied. "I'd rather stand anyway. We have a problem."

"Oh, yeah?" Cooper took another precarious bite, then asked through a mouthful of bread and veggies, "What's that?"

"Officer Jensen just told me he remembered some details of the arrest differently from how he testified," Brunelle explained. "Differently from how you testified."

Cooper shrugged. "Things happen fast. People always

remember things a little differently. You know that, counselor."

"He remembers you reaching inside and pulling Harris out of his home," Brunelle expounded. "Without a warrant."

"Huh." Another shrug and another bite. "Well, that's not how I remember it. It was a dangerous situation. Things happen fast. We were apprehending a murderer. Officer safety, you know?"

"It always seems to come down to officer safety," Brunelle observed.

"Always," Cooper agreed.

"So, here's the thing," Brunelle continued. "I'm going to have to agree to suppress the confession and the murder weapon."

That got Cooper to stop eating. He set the sandwich down, tomatoes and cucumbers falling aside. "Why?"

"Because you arrested him inside his home without a warrant," Brunelle answered. "That's a violation of his constitutional rights under both the Fourth Amendment and Article One, Section Seven, of the State Constitution. The remedy for a violation of someone's constitutional rights is suppression of the evidence. I kind of think you already knew that, or you wouldn't have said he was outside when you arrested him."

Cooper set his jaw. "I did what I said I did. It went down how I said it went down. But even if I did reach inside to grab him, so what? Exigent circumstances, right? I don't need a warrant if there are exigent circumstances."

"You're right, you don't," Brunelle agreed, "and that might have worked if you'd said that the first time. To me and Chen. Or the second time, in your report. Or even the third time, on the stand. But if you change your story now, the judge won't believe any of it, and I won't be able to meet my burden of proof."

"Don't worry, I won't change my testimony," Cooper assured.

"I know, but Officer Jensen will," Brunelle responded. "And I have to disclose this to the defense. It's new information that's beneficial to the defense. I'm not allowed to sit on it. So, I will tell the defense attorney; she will note another hearing; she will subpoena both of you; and Jensen will tell the judge you violated the defendant's rights. At that point it won't really matter what you say."

"If it doesn't matter," Cooper smirked at him, "why are you so upset?"

Brunelle cocked his head. "Do you understand the professional ramifications for you if the judge determines that you lied under oath?"

Cooper took a deep breath, then pushed himself up out of his chair and squared his shoulders to Brunelle. "I caught a murderer. I got him to confess. I recovered the fucking murder weapon. I am not going to apologize for any of that."

"I know you won't," Brunelle answered before taking his leave. "So, I'll have to do it for you."

CHAPTER 15

"Are you sure you know what you're doing?"

Brunelle stood by his office window, staring out at what he could see of Elliott Bay, trying to ignore the thicket of skyscrapers blocking most of his view. It was just after 5:00 in the evening. The time of day when shadows were long and pink, and the sky was heavy in its growing dimness.

The time of day a colleague would swing by his office on her way out.

Or a detective would come over after finishing his own shift.

Or a girlfriend would arrive to meet for dinner.

Or a boss would finally have a break to check in on his employee and the choices he was making.

Brunelle shrugged without turning around. "I think so."

"How can you think you know?"

"I know what I have to deal with," Brunelle explained, "and I think I know what to do with it."

"So, you're not sure?"

"I'm sure it's mine to deal with," Brunelle answered.

"Why just you? Isn't this too important to make the decision alone?"

"It's too important not to." The waves on the bay were white at their crests and black in their troughs. "Justice by committee invites compromise."

"Compromise can be good. Sometimes."

"I don't want to be compromised," Brunelle replied.

A laugh. "You've been compromised before, Dave."

Brunelle nodded. That was true. Too true. "All the more reason not to do it now."

"A murderer could walk free. Is that justice?"

"That's the question, isn't it? Is it justice for a murderer to walk free? Is it justice for a murderer to get convicted with tainted evidence? Is it justice to look the other way when the police break the rules so long as it serves a larger purpose?"

"Can't you just let the judge decide?"

"I'm supposed to decide," Brunelle argued. "That's my job."

"Your job is to convict murderers."

"My job is to seek justice," Brunelle corrected. "It's not to seek convictions at all costs."

"It's not like you're hiding the evidence. You told Edwards. She knows. She can do what she wants with it."

Brunelle shook his head. "No. It doesn't matter what the defense attorney does with it. Harris could have the worst attorney on the planet, and I would still have an obligation to do the right thing."

"The right thing. So, we're back to the beginning. What's the right thing?"

"Justice is the right thing."

"And what is justice?"

Brunelle looked at the thick, low clouds, tinging orange at their edges. A ferry was pulling away from the waterfront. "I think," he decided, "justice is Plan B."

"Plan B? What's Plan B?"

"Ask me what Plan A is," Brunelle suggested.

"Okay. What's Plan A?"

"Plan A is losing the hearing on Edwards's motion to reconsider, the judge suppressing the confession and the murder weapon, and trying to win the case anyway."

A pause. "What's Plan B?"

Brunelle smiled to himself and finally turned around to face his companion. "I don't know yet."

CHAPTER 16

"All rise! The King County Superior Court is now in session, The Honorable Samantha Parker presiding."

Brunelle had heard the click of the judge's chamber door opening and was already rising to his feet before the bailiff officially heralded the judge's entry. Edwards had done the same thing. Waiting for the bailiff to announce the judge was for rookies. It seemed like a lifetime since either of them had been rookies.

"Please be seated," Judge Parker instructed as she, too, sat down. "Are the parties ready on the matter of *The State of Washington versus Kevin Harris?*"

Another formality that Brunelle had become so accustomed to that it hardly seemed like an actual inquiry. Just the first few notes of a well-worn song. "The State is ready, Your Honor," he answered first. The State always answered first, even if it wasn't the State's motion. And it definitely wasn't the State's motion.

"The defense is ready as well, Your Honor," Edwards confirmed, standing next to her client, who had been brought in a few minutes earlier by the guards, just like last time. And just like last time, Cooper and Jensen were sitting out in the hallway. At least they were supposed to be. Edwards had sent the subpoenas this time. They had the same effect as if Brunelle had signed them, but he wondered whether the cops would honor that. Well, he wondered if Cooper would honor it. Jensen was already sitting outside the courtroom when Brunelle arrived early for the hearing.

"All right then," the judge accepted the responses. "This is the defense's motion to reconsider the Court's previous ruling denying the defense's motion to suppress."

Brunelle sat down and tried not to roll his eyes at how complicated lawyers made things sometimes.

"This is again your motion, Ms. Edwards," Judge Parker continued, "but unlike last time, the burden of proof is on you to show why I should change my previous ruling. Accordingly, you will go first this time. Are you prepared to call your first witness?"

Edwards nodded. "Yes, Your Honor. The defense calls Officer Jeremy Jensen to the stand."

Brunelle stood up. "I can get him," he offered. In part to be helpful, in part to spare Edwards the awkwardness of walking to the rear of the courtroom and back while everyone watched him, but mostly to see if Cooper was there yet.

To Brunelle's surprise, he was. Sitting across the hall from Jensen, arms crossed and looking decidedly away from both his fellow officer and Brunelle. Fine by Brunelle.

"They're ready for you, Officer Jensen," he advised.

Jensen stood up and sighed—the first time Brunelle had ever seen him not standing fully erect—then straightened up again and marched through the door Brunelle was holding open.

Brunelle looked again at Cooper, but Cooper didn't look back. *Oh yeah, this is going to go well.*

"Do you solemnly swear to tell the truth, the whole truth, and nothing but the truth?" Judge Parker asked Jensen when he reached the bench, right hand raised.

This time? Brunelle added silently. He sat down and waited for the train wreck to pull into the station.

Jensen sat on the witness stand, and Edwards got right to the point.

"Do you recall your previous testimony in this case?"

Jensen nodded slightly, his eyes downcast. "Yes, ma'am."

"Is there anything about that testimony you would now like to correct or amend?"

Another weak nod. "Yes, ma'am."

"And do those changes or amendments pertain to what happened when you and Sergeant Cooper arrived at my client's home?"

Jensen finally looked up at his questioner and offered a thin, lopsided smile. "Yes, ma'am, they do."

Edwards gestured up toward the judge. "Then please, officer, tell the judge what really happened when you and the sergeant arrived at Mr. Harris's residence."

Jensen took a deep breath and looked up at Judge Parker. For her part, the judge was leaning forward, clearly eager to hear what the officer had to say.

"Sergeant Cooper did approach the front door, and I did take up a cover position at the bottom of the stairs," he began. "But I was actually able to see what happened when he interacted with the suspect."

"And what actually happened?" Edwards prompted.

"Sergeant Cooper," Jensen paused, but then let the words roll out, "he knocked on the door, then stepped to the side so he wouldn't be visible. After a few moments, Mr. Harris opened the door a crack, to see who was outside, I would suppose. When he did that, Sergeant Cooper kicked the door all the way open and grabbed Mr. Harris by the arm. He pulled him out of the doorway and threw him onto the porch. Mr. Harris landed on his stomach and Sergeant Cooper immediately placed a knee on his back and put him into handcuffs. It all happened very fast. Must have taken less than a minute."

"And you saw all of that?" Edwards confirmed.

"Yes, ma'am," Jensen answered.

"Even though at the last hearing, you said that you couldn't really see?" Edwards continued. She wasn't just calling him out on lying; she had to offer the judge a reason to believe this new testimony over the officer's previous testimony.

Jensen nodded and let his eyes drop again. "Yes, ma'am."

At least he's polite, Brunelle thought to himself. A polite liar, but still.

"That previous testimony," Edwards said, "can we agree it was not accurate?"

"It was not accurate," Jensen agreed.

Brunelle hoped he appreciated Edwards was giving him an out by not forcing him to label it 'false'.

"Do you want to explain why you provided the Court with 'inaccurate' testimony at the last hearing?"

Jensen thought for a moment. "I don't know."

"You don't know?"

"Well, I guess maybe I do," Jensen admitted. "But I don't

want to get anyone else in trouble. I made the decision to say things that weren't... accurate. That's on me. And I will accept the consequences."

Edwards grinned and shook her head. "Even now, you're going to protect your own, huh?"

"Ma'am?" Jensen frowned. "I mean, it's not that. It's just—"

"Save it for the internal affairs investigation, officer," Edwards interrupted him. "I'm done with you."

She looked up at Judge Parker. "No further questions."

Parker nodded, then looked to Brunelle. "Cross-examination?"

Brunelle stood up, but only because lawyers were supposed to do that when they addressed the judge. "I have no questions, Your Honor." He sat down again.

"Very well," Judge Parker responded. "Officer Jensen is excused. Any further witnesses, Ms. Edwards?"

Jensen stood up and headed for the exit, completely avoiding eye contact with both Brunelle and Edwards, who was still standing in the well between the witness stand and her counsel table. "Yes, Your Honor. The defense calls Sergeant Cooper."

Edwards looked to Brunelle to see if he would make the same offer to fetch the witness from the hallway. Brunelle wanted to pass, but sighed and nodded to her. He pushed himself out of his chair and followed Jensen out of the courtroom. Jensen had the luxury of hurrying past Cooper without engaging him. Brunelle, though, had to call out his name. "Sergeant Cooper, you've been called to the stand."

Brunelle didn't wait for a reply, and he didn't hold the door open. He returned to his seat at the prosecution table and could hear Cooper open the courtroom door behind him. Judge Parker asked the same question as she swore Cooper in again, but no one really believed his answer.

Edwards utilized the same approach with Cooper as she had with Jensen.

"Do you recall your previous testimony in this case, sergeant?"

But where Jensen had looked at the floor, Cooper locked eyes with Edwards. "Yes, I do."

"Is there anything about that testimony," Edwards held his gaze, "that you would now like to correct or amend?"

Cooper's already set jaw flexed as he clenched his teeth even more. "Absolutely not."

"Nothing?" Edwards asked. "Are you certain?"

"I am completely, totally, and one-hundred-percent certain, counselor."

Edwards smiled at him. "I didn't think so," she said, "but I wanted to give you the chance. No further questions."

All eyes turned to Brunelle, but if he hadn't had any questions for Jensen, he certainly didn't have any for Cooper. "No questions, Your Honor," he anticipated the judge's inquiry.

Parker nodded. "Thank you, Mr. Brunelle. Sergeant Cooper is excused," she announced without looking at him. "I will now hear argument."

Cooper sat there for a moment, surprised at the brevity of his appearance.

"That means you can go now," Edwards instructed him.

Nevertheless, he looked up to the judge for confirmation. She gave it. "You are excused, sergeant. Please depart the courtroom."

It was normal for witnesses to leave the courtroom when

the lawyers made arguments about their testimony. It was doubly appropriate when the arguments would be about the veracity of that testimony.

Once the door closed behind Cooper, it was time for Edwards to make her case. Brunelle would try to win with Plan A. But he knew Plan As rarely worked. That's why there were always Plan Bs.

"Ms. Edwards," Judge Parker prompted, "I will hear from you first."

"Thank you, Your Honor," she responded. She took a moment to gather herself, then pointed a finger in the air and began. "This case presents the Court with a rare, but important opportunity, to right a wrong and hold the government to the standard it sets for itself and others. In this case, the State presented testimony to the Court from two witnesses who, by any reasonable measure, we now know lied to this Court in order to avoid an adverse evidentiary ruling—a ruling required by the Constitution, the highest law of the land and the document these same witnesses swore an oath to uphold and defend."

Brunelle suppressed an eye roll. Edwards was being a bit overly dramatic, especially with no jury to sway. But Parker was nodding along. A bad sign for Brunelle, and the reason he suppressed that eye roll.

"Two police officers came into *your* courtroom, Your Honor," Edwards continued, "promised you they would tell the truth, then lied to you."

Making it personal, Brunelle could see. *Smart.*

"Your Honor made the only ruling available to you at the time and denied the defense motion to suppress," Edwards continued, "but that denial was based on false testimony. That denial was based on lies. And those lies were told with no other purpose than to avoid the very ruling the defense was seeking."

Edwards took a moment as she segued into the next portion of her argument, then continued. "Sergeant Cooper knew he couldn't enter my client's home without a warrant. He knew he couldn't reach in and pull him outside. Or rather, he could, but if he did, then any evidence obtained from that flagrant violation of my client's constitutional rights would be suppressed. How do we know he knew that? Because that is what he lied about. And that is what he compelled a junior police officer to lie about as well. Because he knew if they told the truth, then this Court would suppress the evidence they illegally obtained: an alleged confession and the alleged murder weapon. It was too much to lose. And so, they lied. They lied in their reports, and they lied to you. And Your Honor did exactly what they forced you to do with their lies. You denied my motion to suppress and ruled that the illegally obtained evidence could be used in the trial against my client."

Edwards paused again. She threw a look at Brunelle, although it wasn't as harsh at it might have been, and then returned her attention to Judge Parker.

"This is the part of my argument," she continued, "where you might think I would applaud Officer Jensen for having the bravery to come forward and tell the truth. I am not going to do that. It shouldn't be brave to tell the truth. And it really shouldn't be brave for a police officer to tell the truth. We expect them to tell the truth. So much so, in fact, that when they take the stand and lie, as those two officers did at the previous hearing, all defense attorneys know there is no point to putting our client on to contradict them because everyone will believe the word of a police officer over an accused criminal, let alone an accused murderer.

"So, no, I will not congratulate Officer Jensen on finally, belatedly, minimally offering to tell a barebones admission of the truth, all while even still protecting a fellow officer who chose to repeat his lies."

Edwards glanced again at Brunelle, even gesturing toward him as she moved to the final stage of any good argument, rebutting the other side in advance.

"Now, Mr. Brunelle may stand up and argue that the Court can and should choose to believe the testimony of Sergeant Cooper, and the original testimony of Officer Jensen," she said. "He may argue that the majority of the evidence supports their original testimony, and the Court should find that I have failed to meet my burden to change the Court's original ruling. But I would urge the Court to reject that argument. If this testimony had happened at the original hearing, the State would have failed to meet its burden to show that the evidence in question was not obtained through a constitutional violation. The State should not hide behind a procedural advantage bestowed upon them by their own wrongdoing.

"The Court knows what the truth is now. The truth is that my client's rights were violated. The truth is that the challenged evidence was obtained after and as a direct result of that violation. The truth is, this Court must suppress that evidence. And it is for all of these reasons that I ask Your Honor to grant the defense's motion to reconsider and order that both the alleged confession and the alleged murder weapon be suppressed from evidence at trial. Thank you."

"Thank you, Ms. Edwards," Judge Parker responded in a way that let Brunelle know she meant it. He was in trouble. But he knew that the moment Jensen darkened his doorway after the first hearing.

The judge raised an eyebrow at him. "Mr. Brunelle?"

Brunelle stood up and buttoned his suit coat. Edwards was smart to try to anticipate his argument, but there was no way he was going to argue that Judge Parker should choose to believe Cooper. That was a guaranteed loser of an argument. He had only once chance to win: admit the judge should believe Jensen's testimony, version 2.0, and explain why he should win anyway.

"Thank you, Your Honor." He nodded to the judge and then over to Edwards. "As much as I appreciate Ms. Edwards framing my arguments for me, I must advise both her and the Court that I do not intend to ask Your Honor to believe the testimony from the prior hearing and deny the motion for reconsideration."

"You do not?" Judge Parker interjected, that eyebrow sliding even higher.

"I do not," Brunelle confirmed. "I think it's obvious what the truth is. And I am going to ask the Court to make its ruling based on the truth, and—if I might steal from the witness oath— the whole truth. Because the truth appears to be that Sergeant Cooper pulled Mr. Harris out of the residence without a warrant. And the whole truth is that Mr. Harris is guilty of murdering Amelia Carter."

"Objection, Your Honor," Edwards interrupted. "My client's guilt or innocence is not being determined today. Indeed, we are arguing over what evidence is even appropriate to make that determination."

"The objection is well-taken, Ms. Edwards," Judge Parker answered, "but this is argument, and so I will give Mr.

Brunelle some latitude. I am well aware of the fallacies inherent in this sort of argument, and I am not going to be won over by them as a jury might be."

Edwards seemed content with that response, or possibly just knew it was best to sit down anyway. Brunelle continued.

"Rather than punish the State for what the officers did when they came into this courtroom, I am going to urge the Court to make its ruling based on what they did out at the defendant's residence that night. I believe if the officers had originally said what Officer Jensen said here today, the Court still would have denied the defense motion to suppress. And that is what the Court should do now as well."

Brunelle inventoried the expressions he was facing. Parker looked intrigued. Edwards looked concerned. *Good.*

"Although a warrant is generally required to enter a person's home, even to reach inside it, there are exceptions to the warrant requirement," Brunelle proceeded. "One of those warrant exceptions is exigent circumstances. The police do not have to wait for the delay inherent in seeking a warrant when the circumstances will not safely allow for that delay. In the case at bar, police contacted the defendant within an hour of the murder he had just committed. They knew he was armed, and they knew he was dangerous, and they knew there was a likelihood that his first order of business upon returning home would be the destruction of any evidence linking him to the crime. Time was of the essence. Waiting would have been ridiculous.

Brunelle raised his own thoughtful finger in the air. "Consider it for a moment. They could not have obtained a warrant for the house without first confirming the defendant was inside. But having once confirmed that, they couldn't just wait outside while they took the time to draft an affidavit for a search warrant, emailed it to the on-call judge, waited while the judge reviewed the documents, then finally received the warrant back. In that time, the defendant, now aware that the police were literally on his doorstep, would have cleaned his clothing and skin and especially the knife of any traces linking it back to the crime. Even more worrisome, the defendant could have used the time to flee or arm himself to attack the police officers standing outside waiting for their email to ding."

Brunelle shook his head. "No, the law does not require that. Officers are allowed to act in the moment, in a limited fashion designed to effectuate the limited purposes of that action. They can secure a suspect for officer safety, and they can secure evidence to prevent destruction of that evidence. Had the officers originally testified in the manner Officer Jensen testified today, then that's the argument I would have made. And I would have won. The Court would have denied the motion to suppress because there was no constitutional violation that rose to the level of requiring suppression of vital evidence in a first-degree murder case. Your Honor should not deviate from that ruling now just because you might—justifiably, I would add—be angry or offended by the way the officers' testimony came out in court."

Time to wrap up. The expressions had shifted a bit. Edwards looked unconcerned. Parker looked unconvinced. "The Court should render its ruling based on what really happened out there that day, and what the law really is regarding that sort of high risk, high stakes interaction. Had the Court heard that truth at the first hearing, the Court would have denied the motion, and that's exactly what the Court should do again today. Thank you."

He sat down and awaited his fate. There was a chance. There was always a chance. But there wasn't much of one. Still, it wasn't over until the robed lady spoke.

Which she did. And then it was over.

"Thank you, Mr. Brunelle, for that bit of inspired advocacy," Judge Parker said. "I appreciate both your creativity and your integrity in attempting to base an argument on the new testimony from Officer Jensen. And I think you may have a point that I might have ruled in your favor had the testimony come out that way in the original hearing. But it didn't. And the fact that it didn't is not simply a matter of updating a story. It goes to the heart of the credibility of those telling the story. The truth, Mr. Brunelle, the whole truth, as you said, is that I do not know what happened out there that night, and the reason I don't know that is that I do know the only people who told me what happened cannot now be trusted. I could base my ruling on the version Officer Jensen provided today only if I felt comfortable believing that version. However, as it stands, I cannot believe that version. I cannot believe anything either of these officers has told me. Accordingly, the State has failed to present evidence to me that would be sufficient to meet its burden of proof. Effectively, you presented me no credible evidence, and that leaves me no choice."

So, Brunelle would have to fall back on Plan B.

He just needed to figure out what the hell Plan B was going to be.

"Accordingly," Judge Parker announced her ruling, "I am granting the defense motion to reconsider, and further I am granting the defense's original motion to suppress all evidence obtained after the defendant was contacted at his residence, including the alleged confession and the alleged murder weapon."

Judge Parker pointed down at Brunelle. "I will expect you, Mr. Brunelle," she concluded, "to instruct your witnesses to make no mention whatsoever of the items I have suppressed from evidence. The jury will hear nothing of these at trial and the State will be required to proceed without such evidence. If it's able."

Brunelle nodded. *'If it's able.'* That was the question, wasn't it?

CHAPTER 17

There was nothing quite like a devasting loss in one arena to make you forget about all of the other terrible crap that was happening to you too.

"How are you going to win without the confession or the murder weapon?" came Emory's voice over the car's speaker phone. "What else do you have?"

"Not much," Brunelle admitted. He activated his turn signal to enter the parking garage under his condo complex. "I can place him near the scene shortly after the murder."

"In his house?" Emory questioned.

"Yeah," Brunelle answered. "His house is near the scene."

"He was at home in the middle of the night," Emory translated. "That's not evidence."

"It's evidence that he was exactly where he was supposed to be," Brunelle said as he pulled into a parking stall closer to the elevator than he usually managed to score. "So, that's extremely unhelpful."

Emory laughed. "What else you got?"

Brunelle took a moment to turn off the car and transfer the conversation from the speaker in front of him to the phone he raised to his ear. "They used to date."

"And?"

"And they broke up." He entered the security code into the elevator lobby and pressed the 'UP' button.

"And?"

"And she got a protection order against him," Brunelle offered.

"Well, finally, that's something," Emory replied. "But not enough."

"Yes, well, how about this then?" He stepped into the elevator and pressed the button for his floor. He didn't say anything further though.

"What?" Emory asked after a few seconds.

"Yeah, I got nothing," Brunelle admitted. "I'm in trouble."

"Can you win it without the confession or the murder weapon?" Emory put a point on it.

Brunelle considered for a few moments as he approached his condo door. "No," he said finally. "Probably not."

"Then you're just going to have to figure out a way to get that stuff in despite the judge's ruling."

Emory was right, but Brunelle had stopped listening.

He lowered the phone from his face as he surveyed his condo—and the carnage therein.

Everything was destroyed. Everything. The coffee table. The framed pictures on the walls. The dining room chairs. Everything.

Every single item in his home had been broken, torn, or

smashed—some all three. Every plate and glass had been removed from the cupboards and dropped on the floor. The TV screen looked like it had been struck dead center with a hammer.

"Dave? Dave?"

Brunelle could hear Emory's voice, but he ignored it as he walked deeper into his home. The carnage continued in each room. Bathroom mirror. Bedroom pillows. Everything, shattered, ripped, ruined. Nothing was obviously missing. It was all still there. Just destroyed.

"Dave? Dave, are you there? What the hell is happening?"

He finally raised the phone to his ear again. "He was here."

"Who was there, Dave?" Emory asked. "Who was where?"

"Here, in my condo," Brunelle answered, still dumbstruck. "Larson. He got into my condo. He trashed it. Everything. Everything is gone. I mean it's still here. It's here, but it's destroyed."

"Stay right there, Dave," Emory instructed. "I'm on my way." Then after a moment's thought. "Actually, get out of there. He might still be there. Get down to the lobby and call the cops. I'll be there in fifteen minutes."

Brunelle gave an acquiescing grunt and ended the call. But he didn't make any immediate effort to call the cops or leave his home.

His home.

That bastard had been in his home.

He was stunned.

He was frightened.

But he was also pissed.

CHAPTER 18

Brunelle let himself be optimistic that Larson had overplayed his hand. He had gotten away with the car prowl for a couple of reasons. One, it was a low-level misdemeanor that the struggling police budget had no choice but to deprioritize. But two, Brunelle had destroyed any ability to link Larson to it by touching everything inside before realizing he needed to preserve any possible fingerprints, even if Larson probably wore gloves anyway.

He probably wore gloves at Brunelle's condo too. But burglary was a much bigger deal than a car prowl. Plus, it would have taken Larson a lot longer to do what he did in Brunelle's home than what he did in Brunelle's car. More time for him to leave behind some trace evidence—hair, DNA, etc.— that might link him to the crime. And breaking that much stuff had to have been loud. Maybe one of his neighbors poked their heads out and saw him. Either way, there was at least a reasonable chance that the police might be able to link Larson to the ransacking of Brunelle's condo, and Larson could go back to prison for Residential Burglary instead of Murder One.

Of Brunelle.

Maybe.

But that 'maybe' put a fire under Brunelle, and first thing the next morning, he scoured the courthouse until he found Edwards sitting in the attorney lounge sharing war stories with a handful of other defense attorneys.

"Hey! We were just talking about you," Edwards laughed as he crashed their cabal. "Well, not you, specifically. More like prosecutors generally."

"Yeah," one of them—Mike Kamaguchi—piped up. "You guys kinda suck."

Brunelle decided just to nod good-naturedly and shrug the comment off. He wasn't there to engage in a battle. It was a rescue. Or at least a warning, in order to avoid having to attempt a rescue later.

"It did actually start with him specifically," another of the attorneys—Karen Nichols—pointed out to Edwards. "You were telling us about how you kicked his ass in that suppression hearing with the lying cops."

"Then we started talking about lying cops generally," James Greene put in.

"And the lying prosecutors who lie for them," Ken Helmsted added with a belly laugh.

Brunelle knew all of them. You couldn't practice criminal law for a couple of decades and not get to know pretty much every defense attorney in the county. Mike Kamaguchi was young and cocky, with shoes that cost more than Brunelle's suit. Karen Nichols was nearing the end of her career, one of those public defenders who wore sweaters to court. James Greene was one of the old guard, too, but a private attorney, with an old suit, worn briefcase, and a wreath of white stubble around the back of his head. And Ken Helmsted was a jerk.

Then there was Edwards, the one Brunelle had known the longest. She was clearly holding court, and she had the experience to do so. Brunelle just wished he hadn't been her jester right then.

"Great. Awesome. No, really. Always nice to walk into hostile territory," he acknowledged the situation in an effort to extinguish it. "And who doesn't like being called a liar? But the truth is, I have something I need to talk with you about, Jess. It's serious."

"Ooh, it's serious," Kamaguchi cooed.

"Truly serious," Greene said.

"Truly very serious," added Helmsted.

Brunelle closed his eyes for a moment and sighed. "Can we go somewhere and talk, Jess?"

The others looked to Edwards for their cue. She gave it.

"We can talk here, Dave. Anything you have to say to me, you can say in front of everybody."

Another sigh. *Fine.*

"Ok, sure." Brunelle ran a hand over his head. "Remember that guy Jacob Larson? Shot that guy at that bar? It was like one of our first trials together."

"You mean *against* each other," Helmsted interjected.

"Seriously, Jess," Brunelle opened his palms to her, "can we go someplace else?"

Edwards ignored his entreaty. "Yeah, I remember Larson. He was the one who threatened to kill you after the verdict, right?"

"Right," Brunelle nodded.

"Yeah, I'm not going to forget that," Edwards half-laughed. "He was fucking pissed."

"And now he's out," Brunelle said.

Edwards shrugged. "So what? You don't think he's actually going to do anything, do you? That was like twenty years ago."

"Seventeen," Brunelle corrected.

"Whatever," Edwards said. "He was pissed in the moment. Who wouldn't be? He just got convicted of murder. I'm pretty sure he didn't really mean it."

"I'm pretty sure he did," Brunelle knew.

"You can't be worried about everybody you've ever put in prison coming back to get you, Dave." Edwards waved his concern away. "You've put hundreds of people away. Maybe thousands. It's what you do."

"You could stop putting people in prison," Nichols suggested.

Kamaguchi nodded and pointed at her. "What she said."

"Yeah, no one's going to seek revenge against you if you stop doing revenge-worthy things to them," Greene advised. "Maybe become a defense attorney."

"I don't know," Brunelle responded. "He was pretty pissed at Jess, too, from what I recall."

Edwards shrugged. "He knew I did everything I could for him. You were the one coming to court every day dedicated to putting him in prison for twenty years."

"Seventeen," Brunelle corrected. "Well, I was shooting for thirty, but you got the jury to go down to Murder Two, so I only got seventeen."

"See, he's not pissed at me," Edwards leaned back and grinned. "And I'm sure he's forgotten about you by now."

"I'm sure he hasn't," Brunelle said.

"What makes you say that?" Edwards asked.

"Right after he was released," Brunelle explained, "my car got prowled."

Another shrug from Edwards. "Everybody's car gets prowled."

"And his cellmate snitched him out," Brunelle added.

"Looking for a deal," Kamaguchi suggested. "Snitches are liars too."

"And last night, he broke into my condo," Brunelle concluded.

Edwards leaned forward, and her eyes actually widened a bit. "Did you come face-to-face with him?"

Brunelle hesitated. "Well, uh, no," he admitted. "I mean, he was gone before I got home. But it was definitely him."

Laughter from the peanut gallery. "Oh yeah, that's definitely proof beyond a reasonable doubt."

"Shit, Dave," Edwards laughed, "that's not even probable cause. You're just paranoid."

"Maybe," Brunelle said, "but you should be careful. His cellie said he was pissed at you too."

"As much as he's pissed at you?" Edwards asked.

Brunelle frowned. "Well, no."

Edwards smiled. "I didn't think so. It's like that old joke. Two hikers run across a bear in the woods. One of them starts changing into running shoes. The other one says, 'You can't outrun a bear.' And he answers, 'I don't have to outrun the bear. I only have to outrun you.'"

Brunelle just stared at her.

"You're the other guy," Helmsted explained.

"And that murderer is the bear," Kamaguchi added.

"Jess is putting on the running shoes," said Greene.

Brunelle sneered at them. "Yeah, I got it. Thanks." He

looked again to Edwards. But she was enjoying her courtiers too much.

"I'll start worrying once he makes good on his threat against you," she said.

"You're gonna wait until he kills me?" Brunelle was incredulous.

"I don't want him to kill you, Dave." Edwards feigned concern long enough to add a punchline. "At least not until I kick your ass in the Harris trial."

More laughter all around. Brunelle had tried to be a good colleague, a good friend even. He'd warned her. He couldn't make her take the warning seriously. But he could leave.

"Okay, I'm gonna leave now." He offered a goodbye wave. "I just wanted to warn you, Jess."

"Uh-oh, Jess," Nichols laughed. "He's warning you."

"Yeah, watch out, Jess," Kamaguchi mocked. "The big bad prosecutor is warning you."

Helmsted passed his hand in front of his face as if reading a headline or marquee. "Prosecutor gets ass kicked, threatens defense attorney."

Brunelle looked to Edwards. He hoped their relationship could cut through the foolishness. But she was enjoying it.

She saluted him. "I will consider myself duly warned, Mr. Prosecutor Man."

Brunelle forced a saccharine smile and turned to take his leave. *And I will consider myself duly relieved of any further obligation to watch out for you.*

"And Dave?" Jess called out after him.

Brunelle stopped, then sighed and turned back around. Part of him hoped maybe she was ready to take him seriously.

The rest of him knew better. "Yes?"

"I appreciate the warning, Dave," Edwards said, her expression suddenly quite serious. "And I think I can help you."

Brunelle liked the sound of that. "Oh yeah?"

"Yeah," Edwards answered. "In a week, when we start up the Harris trial, I'm pretty sure I'll stop you from sending another person to prison to plot revenge against you."

"Oh!"

"Burn!"

"You're burnt to a crisp!"

"Put a fork in him, he's overdone and burnt!"

"Murder in the Third Degree Burn!"

Brunelle shook his head at Edwards, then spun around again and stormed out. At least he had new motivation to win the case. He just didn't quite know how he was going to do that.

CHAPTER 19

It was bad enough to have lost the suppression hearing. It was going to be a hundred times worse explaining it to the victim family. Maybe more.

"Thank you for meeting with me again," Brunelle started the meeting.

Probably more.

They were in his office again. It was only the mother, father, and sister this time. No brother, and mercifully no children. But that also meant no chance for a well-timed distraction as he delivered the bad news.

"I just wanted to meet with you to go over a few things and set some expectations," he continued.

They all nodded along. The anxious energy of their last meeting had been replaced with the subdued numbness of the reality of Amelia's murder sinking in. That didn't mean they wanted a conviction any less. If anything, it was the only thing they had to hang on to.

Definitely more.

"As you know, trial starts next week," Brunelle

reminded them, almost certainly unnecessarily. "I'm going to need one of you to testify, right at the beginning, to just sort of establish that Amelia was a real person."

He was met with puzzled expressions.

"You see, I have to prove that the victim was alive until she was murdered." It sounded stupid out loud, but a lot of the law was like that. "It's an element of the offense, so I can't just pretend we all know it. Someone has to say it."

"Okay," Amelia's father offered. "I can do that."

"Great," Brunelle accepted the offer. "That's great. It's also an opportunity for us to tell the jury a little bit about her. Not just that she was alive, but that she was a real person, with a real life, a real family, real people who loved her."

"We did love her," Amelia's mother put in. She wasn't crying, but there was a catch in her voice. "We still do."

"Of course, of course," Brunelle responded. "And the jury deserves to hear that. They need to hear that."

"They will," the father assured as his ex-wife rubbed his arm in appreciation.

"Okay, great," Brunelle said. "That's great."

Now the hard part. He took a deep breath.

"So, um, the next thing," he began. "The case is... not quite as strong as when we met previously."

Eyes narrowed at him.

"What does that mean?" Amelia's sister asked, her eyes the narrowest as she locked eyes with Brunelle.

"It means," Brunelle frowned, "we lost some of the evidence."

"Lost?" Amelia's father asked. "What do you mean 'lost'?"

"Like it's missing from the evidence locker or

something?" Amelia's mother asked. "How could that happen?"

"No, no, not like that." Brunelle waved that away. "I don't mean 'lost' lost. I mean it was suppressed. The judge ruled that we can't use it at the trial."

"What evidence?" Father asked through his clenched jaw. His hands tightened around the arms of his chair.

Brunelle sighed. This wasn't going to help. "The confession," he admitted. "And the murder weapon."

"The confession?" Sister asked.

"And the murder weapon?" Father added.

"What else is there?" Mother asked.

Before Brunelle could attempt to answer that very good question, Father asked an even better question—or at least one Brunelle knew the answer to.

"How did that happen?" he asked.

"Well, you see," Brunelle started, "it's kind of a technicality. Apparently, the officer who arrested the defendant went into his house without a warrant, and that's against the law. It's against the constitution, actually. So, you can't do that."

"But he can murder our daughter?" Mother asked. Those previously absent tears were starting to well in the corners of her eyes, even as her own jaw and fists clenched.

"No, of course not," Brunelle assured her. "But when the police do something against the constitution, the remedy is to suppress any evidence obtained after that. It doesn't dismiss the case; it just limits what evidence we can use. But we are going forward with the trial with all of the other evidence we have."

"Why didn't we know about this before?" Amelia's father demanded.

Yet another good question. One that was difficult for Brunelle to fully answer. He wasn't supposed to tell witnesses what other witnesses had said, and Amelia's father was now confirmed as a trial witness. For another thing, Brunelle wasn't perfectly comfortable asserting that Cooper had, in fact, lied.

"Well, you see, there was some disagreement between the officers about what exactly happened," he fudged. Then, he cut off further discussion, lest he say something that jeopardized the case further. "I can't really say more. The important thing is, you can't say anything about the confession or the murder weapon. I wasn't going to ask you anything about that anyway, but I wanted to make sure you didn't accidentally bring it up on your own."

Amelia's father took a moment to process Brunelle's instruction, even as his daughter and ex-wife looked at him. "So, I can't say anything about those things?"

"No," Brunelle confirmed.

"I can't tell the jury my daughter's murderer confessed?" he continued. "And I can't tell them the police found the murder weapon in his house?"

"No and no," Brunelle answered.

"And no one else will either?"

"Correct."

The murder victim's father looked down and nodded to himself. The murder victim's sister looked away and shook her head. And the murder victim's mother looked Brunelle in the eye, her own eyes glistening.

"That's not right," she said.

"No, it's not," Brunelle agreed. "But it's the law."

CHAPTER 20

The night before trial.

Brunelle had a routine. A ritual, even.

It mostly involved standing on his balcony, sipping bourbon, going over the steps he would take to methodically build an insurmountable case of guilt. There were only two problems.

One, he still wasn't sure how to do that exactly.

Two, he didn't have any bourbon. He hadn't bought a new bottle of the stuff since Larson had smashed his last one, along with every other bottle and glass in his home.

He still had his balcony though. He glanced down at the street below and considered his options.

His favorite bar was right around the corner, but the atmosphere was hardly conducive to thinking, let alone solving the Gordian knot Judge Parker had tied in his case.

There was a liquor store a few blocks past the bar, but it was uphill and not the greatest neighborhood. But mostly, it was uphill.

And then there was that weird little spirits shop down at

Pike Place Market. It was a longer walk, but downhill. (He would ignore the trek back up, for the sake of argument.) That would give him more time to think. The more, the better. He knew there was a way around Parker's ruling. There had to be. Or he was going to lose.

It was a nice night for a walk. Brunelle stepped out of the lobby and turned toward the water. Not that he could see the water from his place, but he knew the direction. He put his hands in his pockets, his eyes on the sidewalk, and his mind on the task of discovering the hidden passage around the suppression of his two most important pieces of evidence.

"The best way out is always through." That was the saying, anyway. Robert Frost. But Brunelle couldn't just ignore the judge's ruling and full speed ahead, damn the torpedoes. If he elicited the testimony about the confession and the murder weapon in violation of Parker's ruling, it wouldn't win the case; it would cause a mistrial. And put the case in danger of an outright dismissal for his misconduct. Not to mention jeopardizing his law license. Nothing like a willful contempt of court to provoke a suspension, or even disbarment. He was too old to start a new career. And anyway, where was the fun in just smashing through a clear and justifiable suppression ruling? The fun was in finding that hidden path, buried in the evidence rules and obscured by the strata of decades of case law, that would allow him, not to ignore Parker's ruling, but to avoid it. To circumvent it. If he could do that, the judge (and the Bar) wouldn't hold him in contempt; they'd hold him in regard. In this particular case, the best way out wasn't going to be by crashing through Parker's brick wall; it was going to be by slipping between a crack in it. If he could find one.

Brunelle looked up. He'd reached the Convention

Center, with its glass and steel arcade-like skybridge hovering over Pike Street. It marked one of several gateways into Seattle's downtown financial and shopping district. That far north, it was mostly shopping, which meant tourists. No local would waste time and money, fighting traffic and pedestrians in search of a parking space, just to buy overpriced merchandise from the exclusive boutiques ringing Westlake Square. That sort of thing was for the guests of the four- and five-star hotels one ring out from the boutiques.

Evading the distracted tourists, heads swiveling everywhere but where they were walking, took Brunelle out of his thoughts. He pushed his hands deeper in his pockets and hurried to cross Fourth Avenue, where the visiting affluent would quickly give way to the local homeless and vagrant. The people who, despite the city's best efforts and their proximity to the aforementioned highest-end retail establishments, defiantly occupied that stretch of Third Avenue.

Brunelle's people.

Well, maybe not his people exactly. He was more on the other team, but they were playing the same game. He was more comfortable in a room full of accused criminals than he ever would be in a room full of people rich enough to stay at the Ritz Carlton for a week. There was a certain respect among those who knew what was under society's veneer. In Brunelle's experience, it was exceedingly rare for any of them to hold a grudge against each other. But apparently it wasn't impossible, or he'd still have an unbroken bottle of bourbon in his condo.

The Market started at First Avenue. He traversed the homeless encampment on Third—complete with tents on the sidewalks and self-appointed guards at the perimeter—and passed by the latest dance clubs on Second, most of which wouldn't last the year, just like the clubs before them, and stepped onto the cobblestones that marked the beginning of one of Seattle's most iconic tourist attractions.

It had been a nice walk, the smell of urine off Third notwithstanding. But he hadn't solved his dilemma yet. Maybe that bourbon would grease the gears. He headed past the fish stands—there was no one throwing fish for out-of-town cameras just then—and into the wooden-floored labyrinth of the Market Building.

Even having spent his entire life in the Emerald City— a.k.a., the Queen City, Jet City, Rain City, and others—Brunelle still got turned around in the tilted switchbacks and dead ends of the walkways that led from the top level on First Avenue down to the bottom level on Western Avenue. The shops were as uneven and eclectic as the corridors. Somewhere in the center, reachable only if one didn't think too much about it, was the comic book shop that had been there before any but the truest fanboys knew who Dr. Strange and Ant-Man were. Branching out from there, along wooden tendrils in every direction, were the quaint and curious, hidden and unique. Candles and crafts. Beads and bottles. Even the old 'head shop' that used to be edgy before marijuana became as legal to buy as the bourbon Brunelle was searching for.

The Market was built where downtown literally dropped off onto the water's edge, so the Market also served as a retaining wall as 'street level' dropped five stories in one block. The route from First Avenue to Western was basically vertical, and Brunelle couldn't help but suspect it was a metaphor for how he could come out the other end of Judge Parker's ruling, to stand in front of the jury, holding the confession over his head in one hand, and the knife that killed

Amelia Carter in his other.

He just had to find his way through the maze.

And to the booze shop. That was first.

Usually, the best way to figure out how to get around something was to figure out why it happened in the first place. There was a reason why law professors employed the Socratic method. Asking yourself the questions forced you to come up with the answers yourself.

Why had the judge suppressed the evidence in the first place?

What was the wrong that the suppression was intended to remedy?

Was the suppression contingent only on that wrong?

Were there other wrongs created by the suppression that might be remedied by admitting the evidence after all?

What needed to happen at the trial that would make continued suppression a greater wrong than admission?

Where was that damn liquor store?

And who the hell was that guy who'd been following him since Third Avenue?

You don't cross Third Avenue without checking your peripheral vision to make sure no one's coming at you. And you don't fail to notice when that person who's coming at you keeps coming at you after you reach Second and then First.

Brunelle clenched his fists and spun around to confront his pursuer.

But there was no one there. Or rather, the person Brunelle was pretty sure he did see for a split second ducked down the other fork of where the inclined corridor split between the walkway Brunelle was standing on and a different ramp to a different part of the Market. He bounded the short distance to the cleft and looked down the staircase on the other side of the wall, but whoever had disappeared down them had done a good job at it. There was no sign of him.

Brunelle straightened up and considered his surroundings, a frown hanging on his increasingly tired face.

It was getting late. The Market would close soon. He had trial in the morning. And he was seeing things. Time to get that bourbon and head home.

The liquor store was at the end of the hallway he'd momentarily abandoned in his unsuccessful effort to chase the ghost behind him. If it had catered to tourists, it might have been called 'Spirits of the Northwest' or something like that, but this was one of those old Seattle businesses that was proud of its dislike of outsiders, not only tourists but especially the tidal wave of so-called 'transplants' who overran the city starting in the late 1980s. They couldn't get away with 'Fuck You, Transplants', but suggested it with the name 'Seattle's Original Spirits'. Brunelle grinned as he saw the sign. He was born and raised in Rain City and could appreciate the sentiment. And the referenced spirits.

The shop was small and cramped, its entrance being the entire width of the store, a metal gate pulled up into a recess in the ceiling. It sported wooden shelves crowded cheek to jowl with bottles of brown and clear liquids, with very few other colors to be seen. Gin wasn't blue in this store.

Brunelle made his way to the bourbon section and selected a bottle of his usual brand. Then he thought for a moment and returned it to the shelf, picking up the bottle next to it instead. Sometimes it was good to mix things up.

Another moment's hesitation, and he grabbed that original bottle too. It never hurt to stick with what you know.

He carried his two bottles of bourbon toward the checkout and took his place in line behind a rather disheveled young man who smelled, not of marijuana exactly, but of several days of several different smokable drugs. He must have run out of the good stuff and was trying to keep the party going with the drug of choice for old people. Like Brunelle.

"Aw no," the young man said, poking at the coins and crumpled bills in his hand. "I don't have enough." He looked up at the cashier. "You got anything cheaper?"

The cashier tipped the bottle to look at the label. "Than this?" he sneered. "Um. No."

Brunelle had sympathy for the man's predicament. And it had just been Brunelle's payday. And the young man and the clerk agreed it was the cheapest thing in the store. But mostly, Brunelle didn't want to wait while the probably impaired young man tried to devise some solution to his dilemma that involved both not having any more money but still leaving with booze.

"I'll pay the difference," Brunelle called out to the cashier.

The cashier looked up, his expression betraying his conflicting emotions over making the sale versus belittling and denying his fellow man. "Are you sure?"

For his part, the young man seemed less than appreciative. He seemed less than anything. He just turned around and stared at Brunelle.

"I'm sure," Brunelle answered over the young man he was helping—or possibly not helping. "It can't be that much, can it?"

The cashier looked again at the rotgut on his counter. "No, it's not much."

Brunelle confirmed his desire to pay the difference and

was happy to set his own two bottles down on the counter as the funky smelling young man dropped his rumpled cash and escaped with his next fix.

"That was nice of you," said the man behind him.

Brunelle shrugged and only half-glanced over his shoulder. "I just wanted to pay for my stuff. Plus, it wasn't that much."

"I suppose that makes sense," the man said. "Especially when you need to replace your own stores."

"Exactly," Brunelle answered. He quickly paid for his purchase, plus $1.18 of the previous customer's, tossed his receipt in the trash can next to the cashier stand, and made his way to the exit. It was only then that it dawned on him.

"How did you know I needed to replace my stores?" he turned to ask the man who had been behind him, but the man had vanished, presumably out of the far side of the store's entrance. The only person in the store was the cashier. When Brunelle looked askance at him, he just shrugged.

He was right behind me, Brunelle realized. *And he wants me to know he can do it.*

But that wasn't the worst part. It was an escalation, a noose tightening. First, his car. Then, his home. Then, his very person.

The worst part was whatever would come next.

And he still had trial in the morning.

CHAPTER 21

The first day of trial always brought out everyone with the slightest interest in the trial. Which was unfortunate because it was probably the least interesting day of the trial. All preparation, no action. Like going to the press conference before the prize fight.

Nevertheless, when Brunelle arrived the next morning—exhausted from a night of too much bourbon and not enough sleep after his run-in with probably Larson—the courtroom was filled with observers. Amelia's family was there, both parents, the sister and brother Brunelle had already met, another man and woman he hadn't and who were probably another sibling and/or sibling-in-law, but thankfully, no kids. One could argue about whether kids should be shielded from the evils of the world or not, but Brunelle didn't care about that. He just didn't want the distraction and interruption that would surely come from two too-young children squirming in the rows behind him. There was an elderly woman seated behind the defense table; Brunelle guessed it was Harris's mother. No matter what someone did, mom would still be there for you. Unless she was the one you killed. Brunelle had tried that case, too, but that was a different story.

In addition to victim and defendant family, there was a delegation of younger attorneys, both prosecution and defense, who had come to watch the old masters. Well, old anyway. Brunelle was feeling anything but masterful just then. Hard to be a master warrior with no weapons. He hoped they would get bored quickly with the preliminary matters to be worked out with the judge that day and then be too busy to return when the jury was picked and Brunelle stood up to give his opening statement.

There was also a reporter in the back row whom Brunelle recognized, sitting next to someone he didn't. He gave a nod to them as he entered, then made sure to check in with the family briefly—very briefly, lest they grill him about his as yet still nonexistent strategy for victory—before setting his oversized trial briefcase on the prosecution table and turning to greet his opponent.

"Morning, Jess."

Edwards looked up from her own extraction of files and binders from her even larger trial briefcase. "Morning, Dave. Last chance to offer me that manslaughter deal."

Brunelle just grinned dryly. "I'd rather lose the trial."

Edwards's smile was far more genuine. "Okay, let's do that."

The secure side door clanked open, and in walked the defendant, sandwiched between two uniformed and armed corrections officers. Up until the trial, Harris had entered the courtroom the same way and was even more obviously the prisoner because of his red jail scrubs and belly chains. This time, though, he was free from restraints and dressed in a suit and tie, and a nice one at that. The public defender's office had a closet of trial clothes, but Brunelle suspected mom had sprung for the suit, lest he look like he was wearing someone else's clothes, like a costume. It worked. He looked like he belonged in that suit. If it hadn't been for the guards flanking him, Harris would have looked like Edwards's co-counsel, instead of her client. The jury would never know he was being held in custody, which was the entire point of allowing him to dress in street clothes. Nothing suggested 'guilty' like a judge holding you in jail during your trial.

Brunelle returned his attention to his materials as Edwards turned to whisper with her client. Everyone was assembled. All they needed was—

"All rise! The King County Superior Court is now in session, The Honorable Samantha Parker presiding."

The bailiff's call to order brought the courtroom to its feet. Judge Parker put it back in the chairs.

"You may be seated," she instructed as she, too, sat down, but above the rest. "Are the parties ready in the matter of *The State of Washington versus Kevin Harris?*"

Same question. Same answers. Same order.

"Yes, Your Honor," Brunelle rose to respond.

"The defense is ready, Your Honor," Edwards echoed.

"All right then," Judge Parker said. "Let's begin with the seating arrangements for jury selection…"

And so the boring began. It wasn't really that boring—not to the litigants. Every detail could provide a slight advantage to one side or another. Every decision against Edwards could be grounds for an appeal should Brunelle somehow manage to pull out a conviction. But to the observers in the gallery, a day of seating charts and time limits and the schedule and procedures for bathroom breaks wasn't exactly what they had come for. It would be a few days before all of those preliminary matters were fully addressed and decided, the jury was picked, and the trial was ready to begin in earnest. But those days passed, and the families stayed for all of it, so Harris's mom was still sitting right behind her son and Amelia's family was still sitting right behind Brunelle when Judge Parker finally looked to the jurors and announced, "Ladies and gentlemen of the jury, please give your attention to Mr. Brunelle, who will now deliver the opening statement on behalf of the State of Washington."

Brunelle stood up, buttoned his suit coat, and nodded a, "Thank you, Your Honor," up to Judge Parker. He stepped out from behind his table and walked purposefully to the spot directly in front of the jury box from which he always delivered his opening statement. He had their attention. He had everyone's attention. Even if the judge hadn't just directed the jurors to pay attention to him, they were on the edge of their seats, more than ready to finally hear the details of the case. Apart from being initially advised of the charge—murder in the first degree—they didn't know anything about what had actually happened.

Too bad Brunelle couldn't tell them.

"Amelia Carter," he glanced solemnly toward the front row of the gallery, knowing the jurors would follow his gaze to the family watching him, and them, "was a mother. She was a daughter. She was a sister. She was a friend."

"And," he turned to deliver another look to someone in the courtroom, "she was murdered by that man right there. The defendant. Kevin Harris."

Good start. That was the big picture. The details,

however, were less forthcoming—having been suppressed and all. His opening statement was going to be shorter than his usual presentation, if only because he had less he could say. But lawyers were paid by the word; he could still knit together something out of nothing. The trick was not letting his audience notice it was nothing, without making any promises for something he might not be able to deliver. So, since he couldn't talk about Kevin Harris, he would talk about Amelia Carter.

He told the jury about her kids. He told them about her friends, especially Valerie from down the hall. And he told them about her apartment. Then he told them about what he saw that night when he himself had the professional misfortune to stand just outside of her kitchen.

"There was blood everywhere," he told the jurors. "The floor. The walls. Dripping down the appliances. But mostly on Amelia herself. Her own blood. Pulled from her body by the eleven stab wounds in her chest, her side, and ultimately her back as she succumbed to her attacker. As she succumbed to Kevin Harris."

Another dramatic glance at the defendant, in his fancy suit.

"You are going to hear from a lot of witnesses. Police officers, detectives, medical examiners, and even Valerie Jones. They're going to tell you exactly what happened. And at the end of this trial. I'm going to stand up again and ask you to return a verdict of guilty to the crime of murder in the first degree. Thank you."

It sounded confident. It wasn't. But the jurors didn't know any better. For all they knew, prosecutors weren't supposed to tell them how they knew the defendant was the one who did it in their opening statements.

So, Edwards stood up to disabuse them of that notion.

"Ladies and gentlemen," Judge Parker announced, "please give your attention to Ms. Edwards, who will deliver the opening statement on behalf of Mr. Harris."

Edwards also thanked the judge. She also came out from behind her counsel table to take a practiced stance before yet another jury. And she also shot a look at someone in the courtroom: Brunelle.

"That opening statement, just delivered by the prosecutor, tells you pretty much everything you need to know about the case," she started. "I don't usually say that, ladies and gentlemen, and I don't say it now lightly. But if you noticed, Mr. Brunelle spoke at length about how Ms. Carter was murdered. What he didn't mention, at all, was how he or the police connected that murder in any way to my client, Mr. Kevin Harris."

That was true. But there was the slightest chance Edwards might step in it and open the door to the evidence she had previously gotten suppressed. It was one thing to say, 'the prosecutor didn't mention the evidence connecting my client to the murder'; it was another to say, 'there is no evidence connecting my client to the murder'. It was a subtle difference, nothing the jury would notice—the former suggested the latter without quite saying it—but the judge would notice. If she said there *was* no evidence, rather than the jurors *wouldn't see* any evidence, then that would be untrue, and Parker might just give him the chance to admit the evidence after all. Maybe.

Which was why Edwards didn't say that. Of course.

"The fact that Amelia Carter was murdered is not at issue," Edwards moved on. "No one is suggesting she wasn't murdered, and no one will argue that. There is no denying it.

She was murdered. Horribly. Gruesomely. In her own home as her children slept in the next room. It's hard to imagine a more terrible way to die. But no one is challenging that. No one is saying that didn't happen. It did, and it's a tragedy."

Edwards paused and also looked at her client, but rather than the accusatory glare Brunelle had cast, her gaze was soft and protective.

"But what is also a tragedy," she turned back to the jurors, "is convicting a man of murder on nothing more than innuendo and guesses. I have no doubt you will hear a lot of evidence of when and where and how Ms. Carter was murdered. What you will not hear is any evidence of how Mr. Harris was in any way responsible for that murder. And at the end of this trial, I will come back before you and ask you to return the only verdict supported by the evidence: not guilty. Thank you."

Edwards returned to her spot next to Harris, who thanked her with a handshake and a pat on the shoulder. His mom looked happy too. Brunelle didn't want to see Amelia's family's expressions just then. Luckily, he had other things to do anyway.

"The State may call its first witness," Judge Parker instructed.

And he'd get to see those expressions after all. One of them anyway.

"The State calls Franklin Carter."

CHAPTER 22

Franklin Carter rose from his seat on the wooden bench behind Brunelle. If there had been any doubt the dignified older man sitting behind the prosecutor was the murder victim's father, it was dispelled as he stepped forward to be sworn in by the judge, his own suit perfectly fitted, his expression determined, and his identity confirmed by Brunelle's first three questions.

"Could you please state your name for the record?"

"Franklin Everett Carter."

"Did you know the victim in this case, Amelia Carter?"

"I do."

"How did you know her?"

Franklin Carter turned to the jurors to deliver an answer at once emotionally controlled and emotionally devastating. "I'm her father."

Brunelle noted his insistence on using the present tense. He expected at least some of the jurors noticed it too. So far, so good.

"I'm going to show you a photograph," Brunelle

explained as he stepped toward the counter in front of the bailiff where the pre-marked exhibits waited to be utilized by the attorneys. He selected one and handed it to the witness. "Do you recognize the person in that photograph?"

Amelia's father had to take a moment. He opened his mouth to respond, but closed it again. After another moment of taking in the image, he looked up again and made himself answer. "Yes. That's my daughter. That's Amelia."

Brunelle stole a glance at the jury to see if any of them were feeling the emotion filling the courtroom from the witness stand. It felt thick to him, but that didn't matter. It mattered if those twelve people to his left were feeling it too. The faces on the jurors nearest him confirmed they were. Good. That was all he really needed from Dad. It was all a parent could ever really provide anyway. Even if the confession and murder weapon hadn't been suppressed, Amelia's father wouldn't have been the right witness for that. He didn't witness any of that firsthand. Brunelle had just told him about it.

Which Brunelle was about to regret in the strongest possible way.

"And that man," Franklin Carter told the jurors, pointing over at Harris, "murdered her. He confessed to the police and they found the knife in his house with Amelia's blood still on it."

Brunelle was stunned. He didn't know what to say.

Edwards did.

"Objection!" She jumped to her feet and slammed her table.

Judge Parker glared down at Brunelle, something close to rage flaring behind her eyes. "Sustained," she growled.

Then, without the need for any prompting from

Edwards, she instructed the bailiff to escort the jury to the jury room for the argument that was about to take place. Well, it would have been an argument, if Brunelle could have defended what had just happened in any way.

"Why did you say that?" he demanded of Amelia's father in a whisper as the jury filed out.

Franklin Carter locked eyes with Brunelle. "Well, you weren't going to say it."

Which was true. But that was kind of the point. It was certainly going to be the point of Edwards's argument. And Parker's ruling.

"Mr. Carter," Judge Parker looked down at the witness, "I'm going to ask you to take a seat in the hallway. You are still under oath, and the lawyers need to discuss the way forward with the rest of your testimony. Please don't discuss the case with anyone until I've had a chance to address you again. Is all of that understood?"

"Perfectly understood," Mr. Carter replied. He stood up and proudly marched toward the exit, avoiding further eye contact with Brunelle. Once the door closed behind him, Parker lit into Brunelle.

"You had better have a very good explanation for what just transpired, Mr. Brunelle." She wasn't quite yelling, but she wasn't completely not yelling either. "Not only did I suppress that information from evidence, but I specifically instructed you to direct your witnesses not to mention it in any way."

"The first witness!" Edwards called out in disbelief. "Direct examination of the very first witness."

Parker narrowed her eyes at the defense attorney. "You will get your chance to speak, Ms. Edwards. Please don't interrupt me again." She turned back to Brunelle. "But Ms.

Edwards is correct. I don't think you could have violated my ruling any sooner unless you told the jury yourself in opening statement. What do you have to say for yourself, Mr. Brunelle?"

Brunelle could only throw himself on the mercy of the court. "I have no explanation, Your Honor. I understand the Court's ruling. I explained the ruling to Mr. Carter and the rest of the victim's family. They didn't like it, but I have no doubt they understood it. I specifically directed them not to mention the suppressed evidence. I can't explain it except to say that I can't control the grief of a father who thinks his daughter's killer is going to get away with murder."

"Objection again, Your Honor!" Edwards interjected. "That is exactly the sort of attitude that's gotten us to where we are now. I demand a mistrial. And I move to dismiss for prosecutorial misconduct."

Judge Parker sighed and leaned back in her leather chair. "Any response to the motion for mistrial, Mr. Brunelle? I mean," she leaned forward again, "can you think of any way, any way at all, that this jury is not irretrievably tainted by what your witness just did?"

Brunelle took a moment to formulate his response. The honest answer was, 'No, of course not.' But he was a lawyer, and sometimes the honest answer wasn't the one that helped your side. On the other hand, he was also a prosecutor. Prosecutors were supposed to be different from other lawyers. They were supposed to seek justice, not just victory. Besides, there was no way he was going to win, and he needed to salvage some credibility for the far more dangerous motion to dismiss the entire case.

"No, Your Honor," he admitted. "I don't think that bell can be unrung, no matter how many curative instructions Your

Honor tries to give, and no matter if no other witness mentions that evidence during the remainder of the trial. I have no argument against a mistrial."

Parker frowned at him, but he hoped she had to appreciate his candor, even if begrudgingly. "I agree. There is no remedy for this, short of declaring a mistrial and starting over with a completely new jury. I hereby grant the defense's motion for a mistrial."

"What about my motion to dismiss?" Edwards asked.

Parker looked again to Brunelle. "I don't suppose you're going to concede that, too, are you?"

Brunelle shook his head. There was warmth in the way the inquiry was phrased, but he made sure to keep even the slightest nervous grin off his face. "No, Your Honor."

"I didn't think so," Parker said. "So, here is what we are going to do. You all are going to leave my courtroom. I am going to bring this jury back into my empty courtroom to explain to them that their services will not be needed after all and to thank them for the time they took and you, Mr. Brunelle, wasted. Then, tomorrow morning at nine o'clock, you all are going to return to my courtroom, and I will hear argument on Ms. Edwards's motion to dismiss. If I grant the motion, the case will be over. If I deny the motion, we will pick a new jury from a new panel, and we will attempt one more time to try this case."

"Thank you, Your Honor," Brunelle responded.

"Don't thank me yet, Mr. Brunelle," the judge snapped back. "When we return tomorrow, I will want to hear not only why your misconduct should not result in dismissal of the charges. I will also want to hear you explain to me why this won't happen again and why it might not be a complete waste of time to start over, given this Court's rulings and the apparent inability of you and your witnesses to abide by those rulings. We will not start this case a third time."

Brunelle knew the time to argue was the next morning, not then. "Yes, Your Honor. Thank you, Your Honor."

Edwards provided similar acquiescence to Judge Parker's instructions, although her voice still carried an edge of righteous anger. Brunelle decided it probably wasn't a good time to try to assure her that he really didn't have any hand in what had happened.

Instead, he packed up his things and headed for the exit. He had someone else he needed to talk to.

CHAPTER 23

"What the hell was that?" Brunelle demanded as he stepped into the hallway and confronted Franklin Carter, the rest of Amelia's family standing behind him in solidarity.

"That, sir, was the truth," he answered.

"The truth, the whole truth, and nothing but the truth!" his ex-wife called out.

"I know that," Brunelle responded. "But this is a trial. It's not always about the whole truth. Sometimes it's about parts of the truth. Sometimes, justice is more important than the truth."

"Do you hear yourself?" Mr. Carter asked him. "Nothing is more important than the truth."

"Winning this case is," Brunelle shot back. "Convicting Kevin Harris is. Holding your daughter's killer responsible is."

"And how are you planning to do that if you can't even prove he's the one who did it?" Franklin Carter challenged. "I listened to that defense attorney's opening statement just like that jury did. She's right. You can't win this if they don't know he confessed, if they don't know he still had the knife he used to murder my little girl."

"I can't win it if they do know that," Brunelle countered, "because if you tell the next jury the same thing, the judge is going to throw the entire case out."

"Next jury?" Amelia's sister asked.

"Yes, next jury," Brunelle answered. "The judge just declared a mistrial. That means we have to start all over again with a new jury. But first, I have to come back tomorrow morning and beg her not to dismiss this case. And the only way I'm going to win that argument is if I can promise her you won't pull that crap again."

"Sir," Franklin Carter pulled himself up formally, "the truth is not crap."

"So, you can't promise me you won't just do the exact same thing the next time I put you on the stand?" Brunelle asked.

"On the contrary," Franklin Carter answered, "I can promise you I will."

Brunelle ran frustrated hands through his hair. Maybe he could try the case without the family. Maybe that neighbor lady could identify the victim from the photograph.

"Well, then I can't call you as a witness," Brunelle decided. He gestured toward the group gathered before him. "I can't call any of you."

"Then who will tell the jury what that man said?" Mr. Carter demanded. "Who will tell them what he confessed to?"

Brunelle pinched the bridge of his nose. He didn't have time to put the family through an entire criminal Procedure class. "No one. Not you. Not me. Not any of my cops or witnesses. He said it, but we have to pretend like he didn't."

"Then make *him* say it," Mr. Carter suggested. "Call the

defendant as a witness and make him say it again."

Brunelle shook his head. "I can't do that. He has the right to remain silent. I can't call him as a witness."

"Well, then ask him when the defense attorney puts him on the stand," Mr. Carter suggested.

Another shake of the head. "She won't put him on the stand. The only way his confession comes in is if he tells the jury something different. She knows that."

"And the only way he tells them something different is if he actually takes the stand?" Amelia's father asked.

But Brunelle didn't answer. He finally saw the crack. It was the gap between what Brunelle said and what Franklin Carter heard. He finally had his Plan B.

"Thank you," he said, more than a little incongruously. "I have to go now. You can come back tomorrow if you want. None of you are going to testify. Goodbye."

He left them staring after him as he rushed toward the elevators, his office, and the evidence treatises on his bookshelf.

CHAPTER 24

When 5:00 p.m. rolled around, Brunelle was still in his office. He hadn't eaten lunch, but had downed an extra large coffee Nicole was nice enough to grab for him at the coffee cart when she made her usual afternoon run. When 5:30 p.m. rolled around, Brunelle still hadn't returned Casey's text asking him how the first day of trial had gone. And when 6:00 p.m. arrived, Carlisle couldn't stand it anymore.

"What are you still doing here?" she asked from his doorway, leaning against the doorframe with arms crossed. "I've been waiting to walk out with you so I could hear what happened today."

Brunelle looked up from his maze of reports and notes and dog-eared reference books. "You don't know? I figured everyone in the courthouse would be talking about it."

"They are!" Carlisle slapped her thighs. "That's why I want to hear it from you. A mistrial? On the first day? The first fucking witness?!"

Brunelle grimaced. "Yeah. That wasn't the best start to a trial I've ever had."

"Was it your worst?" Carlisle asked. "Please tell me it's your worst. Or maybe not. Maybe you've got an even better story about something even more horrendously fucked up. But tell me that story second. I want to hear this story first. I want to hear about what happened this morning. I still can't believe it. The first fucking witness!"

Brunelle sighed and glanced sideways at nothing in particular. "Fine." He gestured toward a chair. "Come in. I'll tell you all about it."

Carlisle jabbed a finger toward the hallway. "Could we do it on our way out? I've got dinner plans tonight, but I really, really want to hear what happened."

"Kristen again?" Brunelle asked.

"No, Natalie," Carlisle answered.

"Ah." Brunelle nodded. "Playa."

Carlisle winced. "Oh God, don't say that. You're too old to say things like 'playa'. And anyway, don't change the subject. Tell me what happened and how you're going to keep it from happening again."

Brunelle took a moment, then stood up to grab his coat. He was satisfied with his research. He could use some dinner too. "You sound like you already know everything I could tell you."

Carlisle grinned. "Yeah, probably. Some of us were maybe talking about it all day."

Brunelle nodded as he pulled his coat off the back of his door and turned off his light.

"Are you going to put the dad back on the stand tomorrow?" Carlisle asked as they headed for the elevators.

Brunelle shook his head. "I can't. He told me he'd just say it again, and the only way I win the dismissal motion is to promise Parker it won't happen again."

"He's not wrong, you know," Carlisle offered. "The dad, I mean. Your jury needs to hear that confession. They need to see that knife. Is there any way around Parker's ruling?"

Brunelle considered his day of research. He reached out and pressed the 'down' elevator call button. "I think there just might be."

"Is it super complicated, totally dependent on things mostly out of your control, and probably doomed to failure?" Carlisle guessed.

Brunelle had to smile. "Yes."

"But it might just work, huh?" Carlisle prompted.

"Yes." Brunelle nodded. "You want on the case now, don't you?"

"With this kind of drama? Hell, yes!" Carlisle slapped Brunelle on the back. "I thought you'd never ask."

"I asked you right at the beginning," Brunelle reminded her, "and you said no."

"I didn't know it would be this big of a train wreck," Carlisle answered. "But we're back in business. Partners against crime. Brunelle and Carlisle, Carlisle and Brunelle."

The elevator doors opened with a 'ding' and Carlisle laughed. "We're going down."

CHAPTER 25

"You think Carlisle came on board because she's interested in the case?" Casey laughed as she lifted her wine glass off the table.

They were at one of their two usual spots they went to when neither of them could think of anywhere new to go to and it was already getting late because Brunelle hadn't checked his text messages. It was in Kirkland, one of the Eastside suburbs of Seattle, just north of Casey's workplace of Bellevue. Cops hated eating where they worked. You never knew if the cook was (a) someone you'd arrested, and (b) especially phlegmy that night. So, they drove separately and met at 'Angus MacFlannerty's Public House and Wine Cellar' on Central Way. The name was a bit long, but they had a huge wine list, an excellent team of bartenders, and complimentary candied bacon. Complimentary.

But still, Casey was laughing at him. "Carlisle is there as insurance."

"In case I screw up again?" Brunelle frowned over his own drink, their own twist on an Old Fashioned.

Casey chuckled again and took a sip of her wine. "Well,

that, too, I suppose," she said. "But no. She's there in case Larson makes good on his threat to kill you."

"Wow." Brunelle set his glass down. "That's dark."

"The truth is dark sometimes," Casey observed. "I mean, don't take it the wrong way. It's smart. And it means they care about this case, and they're letting you keep it."

"With insurance," Brunelle pointed out.

"With insurance," Casey confirmed. "But they could have just given her the whole case."

Brunelle's brow furrowed as he considered his girlfriend's hypothesis. "But I asked her to join the case," he pointed out, "not the other way around."

Casey raised an eyebrow at him. "She waited all day to talk to you? She was even late for a date? She didn't do that because she wanted to hear you tell a story she'd already heard. You're not that good of a storyteller. Hell, she was probably in meetings all afternoon with your boss about getting on the case."

Brunelle frowned. He wasn't convinced.

"Once you offered her a spot on the case," Casey asked, "did she still want to hear you tell the story of what she already knew happened?"

That convinced him. "No," he admitted.

"Right." Casey nodded. Another sip. "Confirmed. Insurance policy. Now, what are we going to order? I can't decide between the fish and chips and the Tuscan chicken. Wanna share plates?"

But Brunelle wasn't quite done with the topic of his co-counsel. "Why not just assign her to the case? Duncan can do that. He's the boss."

"Because you'd pout," Casey answered, her eyes still on

the menu.

"I don't pout," Brunelle defended.

"Um. Yes. You do," Casey looked up to answer. Then, upon seeing Brunelle's expression, she pointed at him and said, "See, there, you're doing it now."

"I am not!" Brunelle insisted.

"Kind of sounds like more pouting." Casey raised both eyebrows and looked down at the menu again. "Maybe I should get my own dish. You don't like to share when you're pouty."

"I am not pouty," Brunelle insisted. "And I'm not pouting now. I'm just... hurt."

Casey lowered the menu and cocked her head at him. "Hurt? Are you kidding me?"

Brunelle tried to keep up the exaggeratedly sad face he was projecting, stuck out lower lip and all, but he couldn't manage it more than another second before laughing. "Fine. I pout sometimes. I can be moody. But I must have good moods, too, or you wouldn't still be here."

Casey shrugged. "I don't know, Dave. Complimentary candied bacon. Complimentary."

Brunelle shook his head at her. "I didn't mean here here," he said, tapping the table. Then he tapped his heart. "I meant here here."

"Oh, Lord," Casey chuckled. "What I do for candied bacon."

Brunelle leaned in and raised an indecent eyebrow. "What would you do for candied bacon?"

Casey took a beat, then grinned at him. "Nothing. It's fucking free."

Before Brunelle could try to push the conversation back to unwholesome suggestions for candied bacon, the waiter stepped up to the table with two fresh drinks on a tray. "Here you are, folks."

Brunelle and Casey both looked at their mostly full glasses. "We didn't order another round yet," Brunelle said.

"Understood, sir," the waiter responded. "They're compliments of the man at the corner table."

They all looked toward the corner the waiter indicated, but the table in question was empty.

"Oh, he must have gotten up for a minute," the waiter said. "In any event, here you are."

"The man in the corner," Casey jumped in, "can you describe him?"

The waiter thought for a moment. "Um, just kind of a guy, you know. Late thirties probably. Brown hair. Oh, white. Um, no glasses or beard or anything. Just kind of an average guy."

"Any prison tattoos?" Brunelle suggested.

"Sir?" the waiter looked at him.

"Never mind." Brunelle waved a hand at him. Then he reached for the drinks.

"What are you doing?" Casey asked.

"I'm getting our free drinks," Brunelle answered, his hands hovering over the glasses on the tray.

"From the guy who swore to kill you?"

"E—Excuse me?" stammered the waiter.

"He didn't mix the drinks," Brunelle argued as he lifted them off the tray. Then, to the waiter, "He didn't mix the drinks, right?"

"Uh, no. No, sir," the waiter confirmed. "Our bartender—"

"See? Nothing to worry about," Brunelle assured his

girlfriend. "Free drinks." Then, again to the waiter. "Free, right? These are already paid for?"

"Y—Yes, sir." The waiter lowered the tray. "Did you say he swore to kill you?"

"I said that," Casey reminded him.

"But yes," Brunelle added. "I mean, probably. We didn't actually see who it was."

"And your description was lacking detail," Casey grumbled. "But the context makes it pretty clear. Do you guys have security cameras?"

"Uh, well, I'm not sure..." The waiter hesitated.

"I'm a cop." Casey pulled back her jacket to expose the badge on her hip. "I'm going to need that security footage. And if he used a credit card to pay, I'm going to need that information too."

The waiter's brow furrowed even as his eyes widened. "I'm gonna need to talk to my manager."

"Better yet," Casey suggested, "let me talk to him."

"Also," Brunelle raised a finger, "we're ready to order."

* * *

As it turned out, the restaurant did not have security cameras. And the Man in the Corner had paid in cash, so there was no credit card information to be had. However, further probing by Casey had led to a few more details from the waiter as to the man's appearance. Enough that Brunelle felt comfortable it was Larson. He also felt hungry because Casey had canceled his effort to stay and order dinner. Something about 'sitting ducks'.

"So, hit the drive-thru on the way to your place," Brunelle suggested as they stepped outside, "or just order pizza when we get there?"

Before Casey could answer, two Kirkland Police Department cruisers came screeching to a halt in front of the restaurant, lights flashing, and punctuating their arrival with a burst from the siren.

"Ah, the cavalry," Brunelle remarked. "A bit late, though."

"On the ground!" one of the officers shouted. He had taken a position crouching behind his open car door, gun drawn and pointed directly at them. "Now!"

Brunelle started to raise his hands slowly. "I think there's been a misunderstanding, fellas…"

"On your knees! Hands on your head!" the other cop yelled. He was approaching, weapon also drawn and trained on them.

"Okay, well, I can't do that but also lay on the ground," Brunelle started to protest.

"Shut up and lay down, Dave," Casey hissed at him as she lowered herself to the sidewalk. "Don't get us shot."

Once they were prone, the officer nearest them put a knee into Brunelle's back and slapped handcuffs on him. Then he pulled Brunelle up onto his knees and turned his attention to Casey. That's when he saw her badge.

"Wait," he said. "Are you cops?"

"I am," Casey answered without moving. "There's a gun in my purse. Don't shoot us."

The officer hesitated, then called out to his partner. "She's a cop."

"A detective, actually," Brunelle interjected. "With Bellevue. I really think there's been a misunderstanding."

"Who are you?" the officer demanded of Brunelle. At least he'd lowered his gun. It was still unholstered, safety off, but it wasn't pointing at Brunelle's head anymore.

"David Brunelle. I'm a prosecutor with the King County Prosecutor's Office. This is Detective Casey Emory with the Bellevue Police Department. And you two are making a mistake."

"My identification is in my purse," Casey said, still without moving from her position with her face on the hard, rough sidewalk. "Next to my gun. Don't shoot us."

Officer Two hesitated and looked back to Officer One, still behind his patrol car door, but relaxing into a more standard stance, gun lowering. Officer One nodded. Officer Two stepped over and pushed Casey's purse away from her with his foot. He crouched down and began rifling through the contents with one hand while he used the other one to keep his pistol trained directly at Casey's head.

Brunelle had never felt so powerless.

After a few moments, Officer Two extracted Casey's identification. He examined it, then held it up for Officer One to see. Officer One squinted, clearly unable to see anything more than the white I.D. in the black holder from that distance, but he went ahead and nodded. Officer Two finally holstered his firearm, and his demeanor whipsawed from menacing to downright chummy.

"Sorry about that, Detective," he chirped. "Can't be too careful, you know?"

He extended a hand to help Casey to her feet, but she refused it. Slowly, carefully, with an eye still on her assailants/colleagues, she pushed herself to her feet.

Brunelle was still on his knees, handcuffed. "A little help here?"

"Oh, right!" Officer Two hopped over to uncuff Brunelle,

and Officer One finally came out from behind his car door. He had holstered his sidearm as well.

"Sorry about that, folks," he said. "We got a report of a dine and dash at this establishment."

Brunelle stood up, rubbing his wrists. He recalled with new doubt the literally thousands of reports he had read where the officer wrote they 'double-checked the handcuffs for comfort'. "You do a felony stop on a misdemeanor theft call?"

'Felony stop' was law enforcement lingo for contacting a suspect with guns drawn, barking orders to get on the ground, and immediately handcuffing. Pretty much what had just happened to them.

"Well, the reporting party stated the suspects were armed," Officer One defended.

"Yeah," Casey grumbled. "I'm armed. I'm a cop."

"I'm sorry, ma'am," Officer Two said, "but you matched the descriptions. White male, mid-fifties, and an African American female, mid-thirties."

"Mid-fifties?" Brunelle gasped. "I'm nowhere near fifty."

Casey finally managed a smile. "Eh, you're pretty close to fifty, Dave. Closer than me anyway, since I'm in my mid-thirties and all."

Brunelle frowned at her assessment, but knew better than to suggest she looked any older than what the unknown caller had stated. Which prompted his next question. "Do you always put two suspects to the ground on the word of an anonymous informant?" Brunelle questioned.

"It wasn't anonymous," Officer One said. "He gave a name. Hold on, let me check my computer."

The officer returned momentarily to check the laptop docked into the permanent workstation that took up his entire front passenger seat. But Brunelle was pretty sure he knew what the answer would be.

Officer One popped his head out of the patrol car again. "The reporting party identified himself as L. Jacobs."

"L. Jacobs," Brunelle repeated to Casey.

"Jacob Larson," she translated.

Brunelle glanced around at the crowd that had gathered around the excitement of a 30-something woman and definitely not yet 50-something man being taken to the ground by two of Kirkland's finest. Larson had undoubtedly watched the confrontation. He was also undoubtedly long gone.

"He's got you, Dave," Casey shook her head. "You're not safe in your car. You're not safe in your home. You're not safe in public. And now you know, you're not even safe from the system you're a part of."

Brunelle didn't have a response. He just rubbed his wrists again, sickened by of the feeling of restraint and helplessness he'd just experienced at the hands of men who were supposed to be on his team. Casey was right. He wasn't safe anywhere.

CHAPTER 26

Nine o'clock the next morning found Brunelle back in Judge Parker's courtroom, his wrists still sore with phantom pain and his head still spinning from what had transpired the night before. His stomach also hurt from the Mexican fast food they'd finally eaten way too close to bedtime.

The courtroom was less packed than the last time they'd had a first day of trial, but both families were there again. As was Edwards, her client, and his guards. And Carlisle. He'd almost forgotten about Carlisle.

"Morning, Dave," she greeted him as he reached the prosecution table. "How was your night?"

Brunelle grinned, Cheshire-like. "Eventful. I'll tell you more later."

He turned to Edwards. "Are we still doing this?" he asked.

"Are you still an idiot?" she returned, without looking up from the notes she was scribbling out on her legal pad. Final thoughts on her motion to dismiss, he surmised.

"I'm not going to call the family again," Brunelle offered.

"I'll get her identity admitted another way this next time."

"If there's a next time," Edwards said. She finally looked at him. "Don't think this motion is frivolous, Dave. That was absolute bullshit, and I don't believe you didn't know there was at least a risk it might happen."

"There's always a risk, Jess," he answered, "but I promise you, I didn't know. If I'd known, I wouldn't have put him on. Like I just said. Now I know, and I'm not putting him on again."

"You're not putting anyone on again, if I have anything to say about it." She turned away again to her notes.

"You do know your client murdered someone, right?" Carlisle jumped in, to Brunelle's chagrin.

"Gwen." Edwards looked up. "Delightful to see you again. Are you here to keep him from screwing up again?"

"Something like that," Carlisle answered. "How am I doing so far?"

Edwards shrugged. "I guess we'll see when the judge comes out."

It was only a few moments before Judge Parker did just that, the bailiff calling out the standard, "All rise!" etc.

Parker took her seat above everyone and got right to business. "Ms. Edwards, are you ready to argue your motion for dismissal?"

"I am, Your Honor," Edwards stood to confirm.

Parker didn't ask Brunelle if he was ready to respond. "Proceed, Ms. Edwards," the judge directed.

"Thank you, Your Honor." Edwards glanced down at her legal pad, but Brunelle was confident that was only to center herself. She knew her argument by heart. "Generally speaking, the remedy for a violation of a court's evidentiary ruling should be limited to the particular violation and should be designed to allow the proceedings to proceed, if at all possible. The focus is on correcting the error, preserving the record, and seeking to preserve the ability of the jury to render its verdict. Hence, for smaller transgressions, the Court might simply instruct the jury to disregard the offending testimony. For larger violations, the Court could provide a written instruction to the jury to disregard or limit the use of the evidence for a particular purpose. In the most extreme examples, when the evidence is too powerful and the transgression too great, instructions from the Court will be insufficient to purge the prohibited evidence from the jurors' minds. In such cases, the only remedy is a mistrial, which is what happened in this case."

Brunelle knew all that. So did Judge Parker. And Edwards knew they knew. It was simply the setup for what came next.

"Normally, a mistrial should serve to remedy even the worst violation. It would have to, because an entirely new jury is empaneled, and those new jurors would, by definition, not have heard the evidence improperly elicited in the previous trial. I expect Mr. Brunelle to argue that the mistrial in this case was sufficient and to allow the case to proceed with a new jury, and that would be the appropriate course of action in most circumstances. Indeed, that's the purpose and utility of a mistrial. But there is one circumstance when mistrial is not enough, when correcting the mistake is insufficient, and the Court should not only fix the problem, but also impose a sanction on the party that caused the problem in the first place. And that circumstance, that singular circumstance, is in a criminal trial, when the mistrial is caused by the prosecution."

Brunelle frowned. He knew that too.

"The reason behind that policy, Your Honor," Edwards continued, "is to prevent the prosecution from attempting multiple bites of the apple. If a jury acquits a criminal defendant, there is no appeal. The State must accept that judgment and the case is over. Therefore, when a case is going poorly, a prosecutor may be tempted to intentionally cause a mistrial, in an effort to start over and correct whatever deficiencies may have arisen during the course of their case-in-chief. In such cases, the courts will consider jeopardy to have attached, and any new trial will be barred by double jeopardy clauses of both the state and federal constitutions."

Edwards glanced over at the prosecution table. "I imagine Mr. Brunelle will argue that the trial had just begun, and therefore, he hadn't had the chance yet to formulate the opinion that things were going so badly he should try to start over. But that ignores how poorly the case was going for him prior to the start of the trial. Perhaps he was hoping I might say something in my opening statement that would open the door to admission of the suppressed evidence."

Well, that much was true, Brunelle nodded to himself.

"But when that didn't happen," Edwards continued, "he took the first opportunity to irrevocably sabotage the trial. Maybe now he'll give a different opening statement. Maybe he'll hope that I'll feel forced to give a different opening statement as well."

Also true, but for different reasons.

"And if that fails, he can simply have Mr. Carter tell the next jury the same thing again, and we'll all end up back here to listen to me argue this motion yet again. Let's not do that, Your Honor. Let us be honest and courageous. Let us call Mr. Brunelle's conduct what it is: unforgiveable and irremediable.

Let us avoid the time and cost and delay of giving the State an unconstitutional second trial. Let us end this now. Dismiss this case. Thank you."

Judge Parker gave that nod judges give to acknowledge a lawyer's argument without betraying any indication of how persuasive they found it. She swung her head to Brunelle. "Response?"

Brunelle stood up and tugged at his suit coat. "Thank you, Your Honor. Let me begin by apologizing to the Court, and also to Ms. Edwards, and everyone else involved in this trial, to include the family of the victim. I have been doing this long enough to know that a criminal trial is a terrible thing to endure. I would never want to inflict that on anyone twice. It was never my intention to do so, and I apologize for not having recognized the risk in advance and done more to prevent us all from having to be here now arguing this motion."

Contrition was disarming. He'd learned that long ago. But it wasn't always sufficient. He'd learned that too.

"But," he continued, "dismissal of a first-degree murder case because of an unintentional mistake at the very beginning of the trial would be an extraordinary and unwarranted remedy, and the Court should avoid extraordinary remedies whenever possible."

He made a muted gesture toward the defense table. "I will not be making any of the arguments Ms. Edwards posited I might make. I will not attempt to justify what happened or diminish the seriousness of the violation of the Court's suppression order. What I will do, is assure the Court that it will not happen in the next trial, should the Court rule against dismissing this very serious and very important case.

"I will not call any witnesses from the victim's family. It

was unfair of me to put them in the position of testifying about the murder of their loved one without being able to, as the oath goes, tell the whole truth. I have other ways to establish the identity of the victim, and I can use professional witnesses to do that. It may weaken the persuasive impact of my case, but that is the cost of my previous lack of diligence. The mistrial not only gives us a new jury, but it also gives me a chance to present a new case, one that will not come so close to endangering the ability of the proceedings to conclude with a jury verdict, whatever that may be."

He took a moment to glance around the courtroom. "This Court's charge is justice, Your Honor. That is my charge as well. I understand the reasons for the Court's suppression order, and I will limit my advocacy to what is permitted by that order, the evidence rules, and the constitution. I have no desire to convict an innocent man by unethical means. But I do have a burning desire to see a jury declare a just verdict in this case, and I ask this Court to allow that to happen. Thank you."

Brunelle sat down again and whispered to his new trial partner, "How was that?"

"Meh." Carlisle whispered back with a shrug. "But you'll probably win. She's not gonna dump a fucking murder case because the victim's dad got emotional and went off-script."

Brunelle gave her a disappointed look.

"I mean, it was great," Carlisle amended. "Very stirring or eloquent or whatever. I guess."

Judge Parker exhaled loudly and leaned forward. She chewed her cheek, and she contemplated how to begin her ruling. Brunelle hoped it would avoid focusing on his conduct. And be favorable to the State. It wasn't both.

"Mr. Brunelle," she began, drawing his name out as she prepared to unleash, "you have, through your negligence, or worse, put this Court—me—in the extremely unenviable position of having to choose between," she gestured toward Harris and his mother seated behind him, "excusing a violation of this defendant's constitutional rights," she moved her hand toward the Carter family behind Brunelle, "or dismissing the case against the man accused of murdering this family's loved one. I hope you can appreciate how frustrated and, if I'm candid, how angry that makes me."

It sounded like a question. It wasn't a question. Brunelle nodded but did not respond orally.

"Ms. Edwards makes several valid points," Judge Parker continued. "The State cannot be allowed to use mistrials to violate a criminal defendant's right against double jeopardy. I have no doubt that without that protection in the case law, prosecutors would do exactly that. It is tempting to use this case to send a message, not only to you, Mr. Brunelle, but to your entire office, and every other prosecutor's office in the state. Do not violate my suppression orders. I don't think I need to remind you of the misconduct that led me to make my ruling in the first place."

Again, not a question. Again, no response.

"But ultimately, based on what I saw transpire, how I saw the parties react, and what you have promised me here today, Mr. Brunelle, I do not believe you intended for the witness to violate my order. I do think you could have done more to prevent it, obviously, but I do not find this was an attempt by the State to manufacture a second, unconstitutional trial against Mr. Harris. Accordingly, I am, just barely, going to deny the defendant's motion to dismiss."

Brunelle let out a sigh of relief.

"Told ya," Carlisle whispered.

"Now, bring in the next panel," Judge Parker instructed her bailiff. "We have a jury to select."

* * *

Jury selection took about as long as the first time. Brunelle's questions didn't change much. He had a new strategy, his Plan B, but if it worked—if he could really get that confession and murder weapon admitted without violating the judge's order—that evidence would be sufficiently overwhelming that it wouldn't really matter who ended up on the jury.

Once the new twelve were selected, it was time to begin again, and for the second time in a week, Judge Parker announced, "Ladies and gentlemen, please give your attention to Mr. Brunelle, who will deliver the opening statement on behalf of the State."

CHAPTER 27

Brunelle stood up, again. He straightened and buttoned his suit coat, again. He stepped out from behind his counsel table, again, and took his usual spot in front of the jury. Again. That was where the similarities ended.

"Judge a man not by his words, but by his deeds."

His entire opening was setting a trap for Edwards. She suspected it, but that didn't mean she could avoid it. She didn't know what the trap was. They both knew the confession was the bait in the center of it, but if he could get her angry enough—as angry as Judge Parker was at him—Edwards might just step in the other trap, the one under the leaves next to the one with the bait.

He figured it was about 50/50 Edwards would object to his opening line. By itself, it was probably not quite objectionable. It brushed up against Harris's right to remain silent without quite crossing the line. A poke in Edwards's eye. When the objection wasn't immediate, Brunelle pressed forward quickly to clarify he was speaking of what Harris had done, not what he'd said.

"Mr. Harris sits here before you, accused, because of what he did. He murdered his ex-girlfriend, Amelia Carter, in her own home, while her children slept in the next room. Judge him for that, for there is nothing anyone could ever say to justify such a cold, cruel, heartless murder."

Again, an invitation to object. Appealing to the jurors' emotions. But it was a murder case. Emotions were part of it. Edwards understood that. She also understood that she held the cards. Again, no objection came. Again, Brunelle pressed on.

"Let me tell you a little about Amelia Carter."

He allowed himself the smallest step to one side. Not a pace—never a pace—but a physical indicator that he was taking a slightly less formal tone with them. He wasn't telling them about the law. He was telling them about a person.

"Amelia Carter lived up on Beacon Hill, at the Bayview Street Plaza, an apartment complex not too far away from the Twelfth Avenue Bridge. She was a single mother of two young children, a three-year-old and a baby. She worked as a nursing assistant at a clinic up on First Hill. Every day she'd wake up early, get her kids ready for the school bus, then take her own bus trip downtown to spend her day helping other people. Most nights, she'd get home well after the kids were done with school, but she and some of the other mothers at Bayview took care of each other, and each other's kids. If she couldn't pick them up from the school bus that day, a friend would. A friend like Valerie Jones, who had two young kids of her own."

Valerie wasn't the trap. She was the decoy. That's where the bait was going.

"Valerie had known Amelia for a few years," Brunelle continued. He gestured at the defense table without actually deigning to look at the accused. "And that meant she knew

Kevin Harris, too. The defendant. The man who murdered Amelia."

Judge Parker had ruled that the cops couldn't tell the jury what Harris said to them. That ruling did not extend to non-governmental actors, like the neighbor down the hall, Ms. Valerie Jones. Edwards knew that. And Brunelle knew she knew it.

"Amelia and Kevin dated for a while, you see," Brunelle explained. "And so, Valerie got to know exactly what kind of man Kevin Harris was, and how he treated a hard-working, loving woman like Amelia Carter."

Another step back in the other direction. Still conversational, still folksy, but not too much. Not a cliché. Just comfortable. Just confident.

"In fact," Brunelle recalled, "when Valerie Jones heard that Kevin Harris was a possible suspect, while she was standing in Amelia's apartment, not ten feet from Amelia's lifeless, bloody body, the first thing Valerie said was, 'Yeah, Kevin Harris could have done this.'"

He stopped walking. "But I get ahead of myself. You'll hear more about what Valerie saw the defendant do, and what she heard the defendant say, when she takes the stand. But first, you need to understand exactly how Amelia died. Exactly what Valerie Jones was looking at when she said that about the defendant, Kevin Harris."

He clasped his hands in front of him—a gesture of sincerity—and recounted Amelia's last hours. "As I said, these friends watched out for each other. Not only did they pick up each other's kids from the bus stop, but they also babysat each other's kids when one of them needed to run errands, or keep an appointment, or on those rare occasions when they allowed themselves the pleasure of going out on a date. The night Amelia died—the night she was *murdered*—Valerie was out on a date, and Amelia was watching their kids. Just a mom, home with her kids, helping out another mom by watching her kids too. One big happy, eating popcorn and watching movies until it was time for the kids to go to bed. What should have followed was a glass of wine, a more adult show, and the details of Valerie's date when she came by at the end of the night to pick up her kids. But that's not what followed. What followed was what the defendant did. That deed you will judge him by."

Brunelle unclasped his hands, and squinted ever so slightly, like he was holding a wince as he prepared to tell them the literally gory details. He held up a hand. "Please understand, Valerie Jones never would have left Amelia alone that night if she'd known what was going to happen. And by that, I mean she never would have left Amelia alone if she'd known Kevin was coming over. Because she would have feared exactly what happened."

Brunelle needed to keep Edwards's eye on that bait. The whole case through Valerie Jones's eyes. So that Edwards didn't see what Brunelle was doing just out of sight.

"Amelia Carter isn't here to tell you exactly what happened that night," Brunelle stated. "I know that sounds obvious, but it's important to remember, in most homicide cases, we'll never know exactly what led up to the murderous acts because the victim isn't alive to tell you. But the cops and the forensic officers and the medical examiner can tell you what they found, what they saw, what they discovered upon examination, and from that, we can extrapolate what happened. And what happened in this case, in the broadest sense, is that Kevin Harris stabbed his ex-girlfriend eleven times in her own kitchen."

Brunelle took a split second to make sure the jurors were shocked by that statement. Eleven times. They were. *Good*. Time to give it to them again in slow motion.

"The first stab was to her chest, up by her collarbone." He pointed to the location on his own body. "We know it was first because she suffered defensive wounds to her hands from trying to block it." He raised his hands as if attempting to ward off a frontal attack. "Here," he pointed to his hands, "and here, and here."

"That blow was superficial. It bounced off her collarbone. But it was painful. Debilitating. Terrifying. She turned away to shield herself," he covered his head with raised arms and turned away from the jury box slightly, "and the second stab landed in her side, under her right arm. That punctured her lung. But it didn't kill her. The defendant wasn't done."

Brunelle turned a little more and spoke to the jury over his shoulder. "The next several stabs were in her upper back, on the right side. Three deep stab wounds, forced between her ribs by the strength of the man stabbing her, by the strength of her ex-boyfriend, by the strength of Kevin Harris.

"Those were deep enough to be fatal without medical attention," Brunelle explained, "but he wasn't done yet. Those were just the first five stab wounds. The medical examiner will tell you there were six more, tightly packed together, deep, fatal, as the defendant plunged the knife into Amelia's back again and again. And again. And again. And again. And again. Until she stopped screaming. Until she stopped moving. Until she stopped living. Until her blood soaked her clothes, and her floor, and her kitchen. Until Kevin Harris pulled the knife out of her body for the eleventh time and fled, that bloody knife still in his hand."

Another poke in Edwards's eye, mentioning the knife. Before she could object, Brunelle clarified that he was talking about where the knife came from, not where it was found. "There was a knife missing from the knife block, and no weapon was found at the scene. Amelia Carter was murdered in her own home with her own knife." A pause. "While her own children slept in the next room."

Brunelle took another pause, a longer one. He was in no hurry to pull the jury out of that blood-soaked kitchen. He let them linger there for a few moments, imagining the scene, smelling the blood, then turned his attention back to Valerie Jones.

"It's hard to say with absolute certainty, but based on the time of death determined by the medical examiner, Amelia's body lay there for about an hour before Valerie Jones returned from her date. It was late. They probably would have let her kids just sleep the night there. Valerie would have spilled about her date over a glass of wine, then curled up on the couch until the obligations of being a mother to two young children woke her far too early the next morning. But that isn't what happened, of course. What happened is Valerie walked up to Amelia's door. She noticed the door was open a crack. She heard one of the babies crying inside. And she knew, she just knew, something bad had happened. But of course, it was worse than whatever she initially imagined."

Brunelle let his shoulders drop a bit. A gesture of resignation, sadness even. "Amelia Carter was dead. Valerie Jones stepped inside and saw the scene I just described. She didn't know what had happened or whether the killer was still there. But she was a mother, and she acted on instinct, rushing back to the bedrooms to rescue the children from any threat that might have remained, without regard for her own safety. She took them all back to her apartment, she called 9-1-1, and she waited, door locked, until the police arrived."

Brunelle shook his head slightly. "You can only imagine what was going through her head at that moment. A million questions. What happened? When did it happen? How did it happen? But chief among them, who did it? Who could have done that to her dear friend? This nursing assistant who spent her days and nights caring for others? Who indeed?"

A glance back at Harris.

"And then the police came. They brought Valerie back to the apartment to ask her what she'd seen, to point out how the door had looked when she arrived, to direct the detectives though her every step as she discovered the body of her murdered friend. Who could have done this? Who? And then she heard the name. She heard one of the officers tell the lead detective they had a possible suspect. She heard the name 'Kevin Harris'. And she knew. She knew. Just like you will know."

Of course, Valerie Jones's personal opinion about whether Kevin Harris was guilty wasn't actually relevant, or in any way binding on the jury. What mattered was the relationship between Harris and Amelia Carter, the fact that they had dated, that they knew each other, that the relationship could have been the genesis from whence sprang his motive. So, the assertion that Valerie 'knew' he was guilty, by itself, was again potentially objectionable. But Edwards had refrained from objecting even once to any of his opening statement. That was good. There were two ways to win an argument. One was to constantly interrupt the other person and argue every point. The other was to save up all those arguments, wait patiently until the other person had finished, then unleash the flood waters of your counterargument. That's what Brunelle was counting on. A flood tended to wash up everything in its path, sometimes even the person who opened the floodgates.

"So, ladies and gentlemen," Brunelle began the wrap-up to his comments, "you are going to hear a lot about Kevin Harris. And you are going to hear a lot about how Amelia Carter died—how she was murdered. So, I remind you: judge a man not by his words, but by his deeds. No one cares what Kevin Harris ever said. But care about what he did. Care about what he did to Amelia Carter. Then, at the end of this trial, I will stand up again and ask you to judge him by his deeds and find him guilty of murder in the first degree. Thank you."

Brunelle turned away from the jurors and sat down next to Carlisle. "What did you think?" he whispered out of the corner of his mouth.

"I thought Parker's head was going to explode every time you mentioned Harris's words," Carlisle whispered back. "I can't believe Edwards didn't object. She just spent the entire time scribbling frantically on that legal pad of hers."

Brunelle nodded. "Perfect."

"Ladies and gentlemen of the jury," Judge Parker called out, "now please give your attention to Ms. Edwards, who will deliver the opening statement on behalf of Mr. Harris."

Edwards stepped in front of the jury box. And Brunelle crossed his fingers.

CHAPTER 28

"Judge a man not by his words, but by his deeds."

Edwards repeated Brunelle's opening line. Brunelle was ecstatic—on the inside. On the outside, he kept a poker face and pretended to be taking notes calmly on his own legal pad. But he knew he'd gotten to her. She had jettisoned her planned remarks in order to respond to his opening.

"Fine," she said. "I can agree to that. But let's apply it to everyone, shall we? Let's even apply it to the prosecutor. Let's apply it to Mr. Brunelle and the opening statement he just gave."

Wow. He really had gotten under her skin. Brunelle began to worry he might not have poked her eye, but rather poked the bear. But he maintained a calm exterior and wrote down the word 'bear' on his legal pad as Edwards continued.

"Later in this trial, the judge will instruct you," she said, "that the arguments, statements, and remarks of the attorneys are not evidence. They are designed to help you understand the evidence, but they are not evidence themselves. You are to disregard any argument, statement, or remark that is not supported by the evidence actually adduced during the course of the trial."

Quoting words like 'adduced' from the pattern jury instructions was a sure way to lose the jury, Brunelle knew. They want to be talked to, not talked down to. Everyone knows you're a lawyer, Jess. Tell us about the case.

"And so it is with Mr. Brunelle's opening statement," Edwards continued. "Judge his case not by what he said to you just now, but rather by what evidence he actually presents to you during the course of the trial. It's one thing to say some neighbor didn't like Mr. Harris. It's quite another to put forward actual evidence that connects him in any way to the tragic murder of Amelia Carter."

She raised a finger to the jurors. "And that's an important part of this trial, ladies and gentlemen. No one is contesting that Ms. Carter was murdered, or that she was murdered in her home in a terrifying way while her children and her friend's children were asleep elsewhere in the apartment. That absolutely happened and that's absolutely terrible. But no matter how many times Mr. Brunelle says my client did it, the truth is, you will not hear one shred of evidence that connects my client to the murder of Ms. Carter."

Brunelle could see the trap flinch, but it didn't quite close.

A little closer…

"Yes, Mr. Harris and Ms. Carter used to date. Yes, they had broken up. And yes, it was hurtful to both of them. Breakups usually are. But there's nothing there to support a charge of murder. Valerie Jones can come in here and say whatever she wants, but it won't change the fact that her words are still just that: words. Not deeds. Not evidence."

Edwards gestured toward the prosecution table. "The State's entire case is based on nothing more than speculation and innuendo. A woman was murdered. It must have been the ex-boyfriend, right? Of course. That's easy. I mean, the door was unlocked, so it must have been someone she knew, and she knew him. Case closed.

"Oh wait, is that not enough? Well, then, let's call in the victim's friend and neighbor to say what a bad guy the defendant is. She never liked him. They had plenty of conversations, and he was always a jerk. But you know what, ladies and gentlemen? I can absolutely guarantee you that Valerie Jones never spoke with Mr. Harris about what happened to Ms. Carter that night."

True. He'd been in jail since then.

Brunelle looked up from his notepad. He couldn't help it. Edwards's foot was right over the trap. She just needed to step down.

"In fact, ladies and gentlemen, I can tell you with absolute certainty…"

Come on, Jess…

"…that you will not hear any evidence at all…"

One more step…

"…about anything Mr. Harris said about this murder…"

Put your foot down…

"…to anyone."

SNAP! Trap closed.

Brunelle couldn't quite contain a small fist pump.

"What are you doing?" Carlisle chastised under her breath.

"Celebrating," Brunelle answered. "When Jess finishes, ask for a recess. Tell the judge you have to use the bathroom."

Carlisle took a beat. "But I don't."

"I know, but I need to make a call," Brunelle explained, "and I don't want Jess to know I'm the one who needs the break. The timing would be too suspicious."

Carlisle shrugged. "Okay." She turned back to Edwards, who was finishing up.

"And so, ladies and gentlemen," Edwards said, "you must judge the State's case not on what Mr. Brunelle promised you just now, but on what he actually does in the days to come. You can only convict Mr. Harris if the prosecution puts forth actual evidence of his involvement in Ms. Carter's murder. They will absolutely fail to do any such thing. And at the end of this trial, I, too, will stand before you, and I will ask you to return the only verdict supported by the evidence put to you: not guilty. Thank you."

Edwards turned and marched back to her counsel table. She sat down next to her client, but their demeanor was different from how it was immediately following her previous opening statement. Edwards was still visibly pissed, and Harris looked concerned.

Good. Brunelle just needed a moment to exploit the triggering of his trap.

Judge Parker looked down at the prosecutors. "The State may call its first witness."

"Um, actually, Your Honor." Carlisle stood up and grinned sheepishly. "I need to pee."

CHAPTER 29

"Larry? It's Brunelle." He was in the hallway outside the courtroom, phone pressed to his ear and hand over his mouth, as far away as he could get from anyone who might overhear him. Especially Edwards, but he didn't trust anyone who might be milling about outside his trial.

"Hey, Dave," Chen replied. "How goes Take Two of the trial?"

"Better than Take One," Brunelle answered, "but I didn't call to chat. I need you to do something very specific. And I need you to do it today. Right now, in fact, while Harris is in the courtroom all day."

"Okay," Chen said. He returned Brunelle's urgency with seriousness. "What is it?"

"Remember Larson's cellmate at Clallam Bay?" Brunelle asked.

"Granzetti? Yeah. Why? Is this about Larson, not Harris?"

"No, it's about Harris," Brunelle answered. "I want you to go into the jail and do to Harris's cellmate what we did to

Larson's cellmate."

"Interview him?" Chen clarified.

"Yes. Exactly," Brunelle answered. "Go ask him what Harris said about the murder."

"His current cellmate?"

"Yes."

"The one who will have to share a cell with him after court tonight? The one who knows he's in for murder?"

"Yes, and yes."

"He's not going to snitch on a murderer who shares the room he sleeps in, Dave. He's going to say Harris said he didn't do it."

"I know." Brunelle smiled. "In fact, I'm counting on it."

CHAPTER 30

Brunelle took a moment before reentering the courtroom to check in with his first witness. He stressed that she could not mention anything about the case other than to answer exactly what he asked her, no matter what else she might have heard. He explained that this was their second and last chance to hold Amelia's killer accountable. He asked her if she wanted to be responsible for her murderer walking free.

She said, "No."

And when everyone had reconvened after Carlisle's fake bathroom break, Brunelle stood and announced, "The State calls Valerie Jones to the stand."

Valerie entered the courtroom meekly. Brunelle had spooked her with the weight of the entire prosecution on her shoulders, but he couldn't risk her going off-script. And despite his focus on her in his opening statement, her script was relatively short. All of that had just been to goad Edwards. And it had worked.

"Could you please state your name for the record?" Brunelle asked after the judge swore her in and she sat down on the witness stand.

"Valerie Marie Jones," she answered.

"Good morning, Ms. Jones," Brunelle greeted her.

She nodded but didn't reply. Because he didn't ask her a question. Perfect. He jumped in.

"Were you acquainted with a woman named Amelia Carter?" he asked.

"Yes, sir," Valerie answered.

"How did you know her?"

"She was my neighbor," Valerie explained, "and my friend."

Valerie was still obviously very nervous. She had worn a nice dress and was clutching her purse on her lap. Brunelle used to tell people to wear what they would wear to church, but less and less people were going to church in Seattle anymore, so he had told her to wear something nice to honor Amelia's memory. That had worked on her, so he was going to file it away for his next case. There was always a next case.

"I'm going to show you a photograph," Brunelle started, stepping over to grab the in-life photograph of Amelia.

But Valerie interrupted. "Oh, no, sir! Please. I don't want to see any photographs. It was so horrible. I've been trying to forget ever since I found her. I don't want to see that again."

Brunelle had mixed feelings about that outburst. On the one hand, she had already forgotten his admonishment not to say anything other than exact answers to specific questions. On the other hand, it made an unmistakable impression on the jurors.

"I won't show you any photographs of the crime scene, Ms. Jones," Brunelle assured her. He handed her the photograph of Amelia, smiling and very much alive. "I'm sorry

I didn't make that clear. Do you recognize the woman in this photograph?"

Valerie let out a huge sigh of relief. Her torso actually shrunk down into her hips, and she let her hands fall off her strangled purse for a moment. "Oh, dear. Yes. Yes, of course. I'm sorry. Yes, that's Amelia. That's my Amelia."

Brunelle nodded, then looked up to the judge. "The State moves to admit Exhibit One."

"Any objection?" Judge Parker asked Edwards. It was a formality. There was no basis to object, and Edwards was far too good of an attorney to simply be obstructionist and thereby irritate the jury.

"No, Your Honor," Edwards replied, barely looking up from her notepad.

"Exhibit One is admitted," Judge Parker ruled.

"Move to publish," Brunelle followed up.

"Objection?"

"No, Your Honor."

"You may publish Exhibit One to the jury," the judge ruled.

'Publish' was just a fancy word for 'show', but rather than stand in front of the jury box holding up a photograph some of them were probably too old to see very clearly anyway, Brunelle stepped over to the projector the court had for the very purpose of publishing exhibits to the jury. The technology was probably a decade old—government, after all—but Brunelle, despite not being 50-something quite yet, was old enough to recall the basic technology of overhead projectors. Heck, he even remembered filmstrips. If it was good enough for Mr. Coe's fourth grade social studies class, it was good enough for the jury. He placed the photo on the projector, and Amelia's face filled the built-in screen between the witness stand and the jury box.

"That's Amelia?" Brunelle prompted her to say it again now that the jury could see the photograph as well.

Valerie had to twist a bit to see the screen, but she did so, then turned back to Brunelle. "Yes. That's her."

"And is that how she looked shortly before her death?" Brunelle had to bring that unpleasantness up again. After all, that was what they were there to talk about.

The smile Valerie initially wore at the sight of her friend's happy face drained away. "Yes."

"Did you see her on the day she died?" Brunelle led her forward through the examination.

"Yes. She was watching my kids while I went on a date," Valerie explained. "I saw her when I dropped the kids off at her place."

"Was that the last time you saw her?"

"Alive?" Valerie had to clarify.

"Yes." Brunelle wanted her to have to.

"Yes, that was the last time I saw her alive."

"And you were the first person to find her after she had been murdered," Brunelle continued. "Isn't that correct?"

"As far as I know," Valerie answered. "I mean, except for the guy who did it." She punctuated that sentiment with a look over at Harris.

Nice touch, Brunelle thought. But again, outside of his question. He needed to be efficient with his examination and get her off the stand before she said something that caused a mistrial again.

"I promised you I wouldn't show you any photographs of the crime scene," Brunelle said.

"Thank you," Valerie responded.

Brunelle nodded. "And I won't need you to describe what you saw exactly. The officers who responded can describe the scene. But can you tell me what you did when you came home from your date?"

So, Valerie explained it pretty much the same way she'd told Chen that night, and the way Brunelle had told the jury that morning. She came home. The door was ajar. The baby was crying. She went inside. She saw what she didn't want to see again. She grabbed the kids, and she went to her apartment, and she called 9-1-1.

"Did you notice anyone else in the apartment, other than the kids?"

Valerie shook her head. "No. I mean, I can't say for sure no one was there, but I didn't see anyone. I was focused on getting the kids and getting out."

"Of course, of course," Brunelle acknowledged. "And did you ever notice anyone suspicious hanging around or running away or anything like that when you got home from your date?"

"No, nothing like that," Valerie answered. "When I got back, I was just thinking about my date and seeing my kids again. And after I saw what I saw, I was just thinking about protecting the babies and calling the police."

Brunelle nodded several times. One last area to cover. The most important one. Like Edwards said, no one was contesting that Amelia was murdered. The trick was connecting Harris to it.

"Are you acquainted with the defendant, Kevin Harris?" he asked.

"Acquainted?" Valerie asked with obvious derision.

"Yeah, I'm acquainted with him. I wish I wasn't, but I am."

Another nod from Brunelle. "And how did you come to be acquainted with him?"

"Amelia made the mistake of dating him for a while," Valerie answered. "I told her he was trouble, but she wouldn't listen. She had to find out for herself." Then, realizing the implication of what she'd said, a sob suddenly escaped her mouth. "Oh, God. I didn't, I didn't mean it that way. It wasn't Amelia's fault."

"Of course not," Brunelle consoled.

"It's his fault!" Valerie pointed at Harris, hand shaking. "Not her fault she got murdered. Not Amelia's fault. His fault!"

Brunelle pursed his lips. He liked the drama, and he loved the sentiment, but the problem was that Valerie didn't actually know it was Harris's fault. Not firsthand. She didn't witness the murder. She was basing her conclusion on her own opinion of the man. And quite possibly—probably, even—on what she had heard from the family, to wit: that Harris confessed and they found him with the murder weapon. Brunelle wanted to explore a bit more about how Harris had treated Amelia prior to the murder, but he just couldn't risk another outburst, another mistrial.

And there were worse ways to end the examination of the first witness than a crying witness pointing at the defendant and calling him a murderer.

"Thank you, Ms. Jones," Brunelle said. "I have no further questions for you."

Valerie rubbed the back of a hand under her nose. "Can I go now?"

"Not yet," Judge Parker leaned over to inform her. "The defense attorney may have some questions for you."

Valerie's eyes narrowed and her jaw set as she glared over at Edwards. "Oh."

Edwards stood up and slowly approached the witness stand.

"Ms. Jones," she said, "I am going to ask you a few yes-or-no questions. I want you to answer either 'yes' or 'no'. Please do not try to add anything. If you don't think you can answer with just a 'yes' or a 'no', then please tell me, and I will rephrase the question. Do you understand?"

Valerie's eyes narrowed even further. After a moment, she conceded with a, "Yes."

"Good," Edwards said. "Now, the first question. You did not actually witness the murder, did you?"

Valerie hesitated.

"Remember," Edwards interjected. "Yes or no."

"No," Valerie admitted.

"And you did not see anyone else in or around Ms. Carter's apartment other than the children you removed from there, did you?"

Another hesitation, obviously from having to agree with the lawyer defending the man who had murdered her friend. "No."

"And finally," Edwards said, "you have not spoken to Mr. Harris at all in any way since you returned home from your date and found Ms. Carter murdered, have you?"

Valerie frowned at Edwards, then scowled at Harris. "I have nothing to say to that murderer."

Edwards kept her composure. "Is that a 'no', Ms. Jones?"

Valerie sneered at her. "No. I haven't spoken with him since he murdered Amelia."

Edwards looked up at the judge. "I'd ask that the

witness's last response be stricken after the word 'no'."

Judge Parker nodded and addressed the jurors. "The jury will disregard everything in the witness's last answer after the word 'no'."

"No further questions," Edwards told the judge, and she returned to her seat.

"Any redirect examination?" Judge Parker almost dared Brunelle.

Under different circumstances—like a not-suppressed confession and not-mistried first trial—Brunelle would have relished the opportunity to allow a witness like Valerie Jones to breathe life into the proceedings. But it wasn't different circumstances.

"No, Your Honor," Brunelle answered. "The witness may be excused."

He sat down again.

"You dodged another bullet," Carlisle quipped. "I was sure she was going to blurt out something about the confession. You've got nine lives or something."

"Or something," Brunelle answered. "Anyway, it's your turn to dodge some bullets. Good luck."

"Please," Carlisle said. "I eat bullets for breakfast."

"The State may call its next witness," the judge invited.

Carlisle stood up to reply. "The State calls Dr. Sharon Roe."

CHAPTER 31

Carlisle may have eaten bullets for breakfast, but doing the direct examination of the medical examiner in a murder trial was a piece of cake. With ice cream. And whipped cream. And at least one of the frosting roses.

The M.E. had the most interesting testimony and was pretty much unassailable on cross-examination. Plus, Edwards wasn't going to claim Amelia Carter didn't die from eleven stab wounds to her front, side, and back. She might not cross Dr. Roe at all.

Dr. Roe entered the courtroom and walked directly to the judge to be sworn in. She'd done this before. A lot. Carlisle hadn't done as many trials yet, but she knew the routine. She waited for the good doctor to be seated on the witness stand, then began her direct examination.

"Please state your name and title for the record."

"Dr. Sharon Elizabeth Roe." All that experience testifying led her to deliver her answer directly to the jurors, not back at Carlisle.

"How are you employed, doctor?"

"I am an Assistant Medical Examiner at the King County Medical Examiner's Office," she told the jury.

"Did you conduct the autopsy of Amelia Carter, in relation to the case of *The State of Washington versus Kevin Harris?*"

A sharp nod to the jury box. "I did."

Brunelle watched the beginning of the testimony—the beginning of anything was usually at least a little bit interesting—but as Carlisle started into Dr. Roe's degrees, residencies, and awards, he lowered his eyes to his legal pad and let his mind wander a bit. It wasn't from lack of interest in the case. To the contrary, it was because of his interest in winning.

Dr. Roe's testimony was necessary, but insufficient. Brunelle knew exactly what Edwards's cross would be. The same as it had been for Valerie Jones. The same as it would be for every one of their witnesses.

You didn't see the murder, did you?

You don't know who killed her, do you?

You can't say my client committed the murder, can you?

Or some variation on that theme.

Brunelle needed Dr. Roe to testify as to what caused Amelia Carter's death. But someone else would have to testify as to who caused it. She was filler. But good filler. It would be interesting, informative, and heart-wrenching. And it would take the better part of a full day, maybe two. And that was the real point. It would give Chen the time needed to get that witness who could answer Edwards's question with, '*Yes, Kevin Harris murdered Amelia Carter.*'

Brunelle looked up again. Dr. Roe was explaining to the jury the etymological origin of the word 'autopsy'. He leaned back and covered his grin with his hand. Chen was going to have plenty of time.

CHAPTER 32

It would actually be several days before Chen testified. After Dr. Roe, Brunelle and Carlisle put on a series of cops and forensics officers who talked about the processing of the crime scene. It was then that they showed the jury those photos Valerie Jones had begged not to see. Photographs couldn't truly convey the horror of a murder scene, especially one as bloody as Amelia Carter's, but they could come close. Especially to a jury box full of retired teachers, airplane mechanics, and techies.

By the time Chen took the stand, the conversation with Harris's current cellmate had been completed, documented, and delivered to Edwards in compliance with the prosecution's discovery obligation under the criminal court rules. That didn't mean Edwards wasn't pissed.

"This is outrageous, Your Honor," she complained the morning after Brunelle handed her the report in open court, at the end of the day's proceedings with Chen scheduled to testify first thing the next morning. "This is late discovery. I can't think of anything later than in the middle of the State's case-in-chief. I've barely had time to read this. The Court should not allow any testimony as to anything contained in this report."

That was her real complaint. If Brunelle had handed her a report with nothing particularly damaging in it, she wouldn't have cared about it being late. She would have dealt with it in stride, like the seasoned professional she was. That she was fighting against the contents of the report let everyone know, including Judge Parker, that her true fear lay in the words of the report, not its timing.

The jury was locked away in the jury room. Chen was waiting in the hallway. The families were again seated in their usual seats. A few random members of the public filled the back rows of the gallery. And Judge Parker leaned forward to ask the question that really mattered. "What's in the report?"

Brunelle stood to answer, but Edwards beat him to it. With her own spin, of course.

"Apparently, after opening statements, Mr. Brunelle instructed Detective Chen to interview my client's current cellmate in the King County Jail, even as we all were convened here in your courtroom, Your Honor. Ostensibly, this was in response to my assertion in my opening statement that my client," she flipped to the relevant page of the report, "'never said anything to anyone about the murder'. Which, by the way, is not what I said. I was very careful in my choice of words. I said the jury would not hear any evidence of anything he said to anyone about the murder. That was true and accurate, made in reliance on the Court's ruling suppressing his statements about the murder. If I'd told them he never spoke to anyone about the murder, that would not have been true, and I'm sure Mr. Brunelle would have argued that I had opened the door to the confession. That, of course, ignores the ample case law that an opening statement by an attorney cannot alone open the door to admit otherwise inadmissible evidence, but—"

"Thank you, Ms. Edwards," Judge Parker interrupted. "I'm familiar with the case law, as, I expect, is Mr. Brunelle."

Brunelle was. Barring some outrageous lie like, 'The police didn't even try to talk to my client' or something, Edwards herself couldn't open the door to allowing the confession in. But she could open the door to other evidence that could in turn, just maybe, open that second door Brunelle so desperately wanted to lead the jury through.

"I take it," Judge Parker surmised, "your client's cellmate divulged some statements made by your client regarding this case?"

"Allegedly made," Edwards responded. "And yes. And now Mr. Brunelle wants to call that witness to tell the jury what my client allegedly said. This is in complete violation, not only of the discovery rules, but the spirit of the Court's ruling that my client's statements regarding the murder should be suppressed."

Judge Parker tilted her head. "I'm not sure my ruling was quite that broad." She looked to the prosecution table. "Mr. Brunelle, any response? How is this not late discovery, and why should I not suppress it for violation of the court rules?"

"It's not late, Your Honor," Brunelle stood again, "because it just happened. I couldn't have provided it to Ms. Edwards prior to the start of trial because it didn't exist yet. As soon as it happened, and Detective Chen completed his report, I provided it to Ms. Edwards. I also made a point of timing Detective Chen's testimony so that she would have an entire evening and night to review the report prior to him taking the stand."

"We are still well into the trial, Mr. Brunelle," Judge Parker reminded him. "How might this information have impacted Ms. Edwards's opening statement? How does this not prejudice her representation of her client?"

"Yes!" Edwards interjected. "Exactly."

Judge Parker shot Edwards a glance to remind her to wait her turn to speak, then looked back to Brunelle for his answer.

"It doesn't prejudice her opening statement because it was prompted by that opening statement, Your Honor," Brunelle argued. "The beginning of a trial isn't some magical event that prevents further investigation into a case. If anything, such an endeavor is likely to unearth new areas of inquiry, new leads as those closest to the case take the stand and recount what they know about the case. It would be the exception, I should think, to have a trial that didn't reveal at least some surprises along the way. I wouldn't be doing my job if I didn't follow up on those leads, in an effort to uncover the truth and help the jury reach the proper verdict."

"You mean a conviction," Edwards grumbled.

"If the verdict form fits," Brunelle returned.

"Quiet, both of you," Parker admonished. She leaned back and rubbed a hand over her chin. "Your statement to the jury was a bit broader than my ruling, Ms. Edwards. I noticed it at the time and wondered whether Mr. Brunelle would object. It appears he decided to try to use it against you instead."

Brunelle couldn't argue with that.

The judge leaned forward again. "What exactly did this cellmate claim Mr. Harris said about the murder?"

Edwards flipped through the report again. Brunelle already knew the answer, but he let Edwards deliver the information.

"Um, let me see," Edwards said. "Okay, here it is.

Detective Chen wrote, 'Dudley—that's his cellmate, William Dudley—said that Harris came back from court agitated and excited. Harris told Dudley, 'I'm gonna beat this fucking murder case. There's no way they convict me. I'm gonna walk.'"

"Keep reading," Brunelle prompted Edwards.

"I was about to," she shot back. She read again from the report. "'Dudley asked Harris why he was going to beat the case, and Harris slapped the wall and said, 'Because I didn't fucking kill her, dumb ass!'"

Judge Parker raised an eyebrow and looked to Brunelle. "That's what you want admitted?"

Brunelle nodded. "Yes, Your Honor."

Parker chewed her cheek for a moment. "That doesn't seem very helpful to your case," she opined.

Brunelle shrugged. "It depends, Your Honor. There's a lot of context around all that. I think the jury deserves to know that what Ms. Edwards told them wasn't accurate."

"Ms. Edwards isn't on trial, Mr. Brunelle," the judge reminded him.

"No, but her client is, and she speaks for him," Brunelle responded. "She can't tell the jury the State doesn't have certain evidence and then complain when we produce it. It's one thing if certain evidence has been suppressed, but that's not the case here. There's nothing inherently inadmissible about this evidence. It hasn't been suppressed, and by rule, it's not hearsay. When the State offers a statement of the defendant, it's not subject to the usual hearsay rules. We all know that. This is standard evidence, of a type regularly admitted in criminal trials. I would apologize that it wasn't provided sooner, but again, it didn't exist sooner. Ms. Edwards is an experienced attorney; she got this information a full day ago; and while I believe the evidence is helpful to the State, it's not like it's a bombshell confession. I agree something like that might warrant a different approach, but that's not what we have here."

Judge Parker chewed her cheek again and looked over to Edwards. "You don't want the jurors to hear that evidence? Seems like it could be helpful to you."

Edwards frowned at the report in her hand. "Maybe, Your Honor. But as I said, this was just given to me, and I haven't had the time to fully appreciate the consequences of this potential evidence."

"Are you asserting that your client didn't say the statements attributed to him by Mr. Dudley?" Judge Parker asked.

"With all due respect, Your Honor," Edwards answered, "I don't think that's really relevant. It's the principle of the matter."

Judge Parker accepted Edwards's assertion without commenting on it. She took a few moments to stroke her chin again and chew her cheek again and let those gears behind her eyes turn. Brunelle was still standing. He didn't dare move lest he disturb her thoughts. Finally, she leaned forward again.

"I'm going to allow the evidence," she declared. "I agree that it's late in the common sense of that word, but I don't believe it's late for the purposes of the court rules. Mr. Brunelle turned it over as soon as it was ready, and he is correct that he is under no obligation to cease investigation of a case just because the trial has commenced. Quite the opposite is likely to be true sometimes, although I'm not sure this is the ground-shaking revelation the parties seem to think it is. Still, I will allow it. But Mr. Brunelle," she shook her head at him, "be careful what you wish for."

Brunelle smiled up at the judge. "I always am, Your Honor."

CHAPTER 33

Chen was quick. Not so much because he didn't have a lot to say, but because Brunelle was impatient to get Dudley on and off the stand before Parker changed her mind.

Carlisle had done a lot of the preceding cop and forensic witnesses, but Brunelle needed to do Chen's examination himself. And Dudley's. And, if it worked, the one last witness they would call after Dudley.

So Brunelle led Chen through the usual dog-and-pony show. Name, rank, and badge number. Years on the force. Years as a detective. Years as a homicide detective. The callout on this case. The scene. The interview of Valerie Jones. And then, when it would have been an abrupt, almost puzzling end to his testimony as he completely failed to mention any effort whatsoever to locate, contact, or interrogate Harris, Brunelle moved to the real reason Chen was there.

"Have you had a chance, during your investigation," he asked, as if he didn't already know the answer, "to speak to anyone who spoke to Mr. Harris about the murder of Amelia Carter?"

At the beginning of the trial, that answer would have been, 'No', even though 'the whole truth' was 'yes'. Lawyers had a different meaning for 'the whole truth' and cops were obliged to follow the lawyers. But Judge Parker was allowing Chen to tell 'some of the truth'.

"Yes," Chen answered.

Brunelle glanced at the jurors to see if there was any ripple of surprise through their ranks, but Edwards's opening statement was so long ago, and her wording so exact, that none of them seemed impressed by what he felt should have been a stunning revelation.

"And who was that?"

Again, the whole truth would have included Sgt. Cooper and Officer Jensen. But the some of the truth that was allowed was, "William Dudley."

"When did you speak with Mr. Dudley?"

"Just a few days ago," Chen admitted.

"And did you ascertain how Mr. Dudley and Mr. Harris are acquainted?"

"Yes." Chen knew this was another one of those 'some of the truth' moments. The jury wasn't allowed to know Harris was being held in custody. "They were roommates."

Not untrue, just not complete.

"Okay, thanks," Brunelle acknowledged the answer. Then the final question to set up Dudley. Dudley could say what Harris told him. But Chen couldn't say what Dudley said Harris said because that was too far removed and would be blocked by Edwards's absolutely certain hearsay objection. "And, yes or no, did Mr. Dudley tell you what Mr. Harris told him about the murder of Amelia Carter?"

Chen turned to the jurors to answer. "Yes, he did."

"Thank you, Detective. No further questions."

Brunelle sat down and Edwards stood up. She had the copy of Chen's report in her hands and raised it at him like a weapon. "You wrote a report about your conversation with Mr. Dudley, isn't that correct?"

"Yes, ma'am," Chen answered.

"And in that report you wrote down everything Mr. Dudley claimed Mr. Harris told him about the murder, is that right?"

Again, "Yes, ma'am."

"Please tell the jury everything Mr. Dudley claimed my client said about the murder."

It turned out Brunelle would have to make that hearsay objection. "Objection, Your Honor. Calls for hearsay."

Judge Parker looked down at Brunelle with an obvious, 'Are you kidding me?' expression, but then she caught herself and regained her features, lest any of the jurors see her opinion on her face. It was a well taken objection. She had no choice.

"Objection sustained," Judge Parker ruled. "This witness cannot testify as to what other witnesses told him the defendant may have said."

Edwards nodded, clearly frustrated, a little puzzled, but willing to be patient. Everyone knew Dudley was next. "Then no further questions for this witness, Your Honor."

She returned to her seat and Judge Parker asked Brunelle, "Any redirect examination?"

"No, Your Honor. The witness may be excused," Brunelle answered. He was as eager as anyone to get Chen off the stand and Dudley on it. Although that was going to require a recess. Dudley was still being held in custody himself. He needed to be brought into court by corrections officers, just like

Harris, and he needed to be dressed in street clothes as well, just in case the soon-to-be four armed jail guards didn't tip off to the jury that *someone* in the courtroom was being held in the jail.

Parker called for the recess, and after the jurors were securely behind their closed jury room door, the bailiff called the jail and requested transport of the next witness. It took longer than it should have—most things do—but eventually William Dudley was seated on the witness stand, a guard was stationed directly behind him pretending to be just another bailiff, the jury was brought out, and Brunelle announced, "The State calls William Dudley to the stand."

CHAPTER 34

Dudley looked nervous. In fact, beads of sweat were clearly visible on his freckled forehead, dripping down from a buzzcut of prematurely receding red hair. Sweat stains spread out from under his arms, and his pink-rimmed eyes darted around the courtroom, but managed to avoid Harris, who was staring straight through him.

Parker had him stand and be sworn in from the witness stand. The jurors undoubtedly noticed the difference in Dudley's entrance as compared to every other witness they'd heard from over the previous weeks, but there was nothing else to be done. Brunelle was happy to leave them to draw their own, very obvious conclusions.

"Could you please state your name for the record?" Brunelle began.

"Um." Dudley's eyes darted over to the jury, up to the judge, and back to Brunelle. "William Dudley. William Alan Dudley."

"You are acquainted with the defendant, Mr. Kevin Harris, is that correct?" Brunelle was going to have to lead him a bit to avoid mentioning exactly how they knew each other. "It's a yes-or-no question."

Dudley nodded. "Yes."

"Is it safe to say the two of you were roommates at one point?" Brunelle suggested.

Dudley thought for a moment. He looked again at the jury before answering to Brunelle. "Sure."

"Do you recall ever having a conversation with Mr. Harris about the murder of Amelia Carter?"

Dudley frowned. "Was that her name? Amelia, uh, whatever you just said?"

"Yes," Brunelle frowned as well. "Her name was Amelia Carter."

"Um, then, yes," Dudley confirmed. "Yes, I recall that. I mean, it was a short conversation, but yes."

Brunelle picked up a copy of Chen's report and turned to the appropriate page. "Is it true that Mr. Harris told you, and I quote, 'I'm going to beat this fucking murder case'?"

Dudley nodded. "Yeah, that sounds about right."

"He said that?" Brunelle wanted to nail it down solid. As solidly as he could with a nervous, sweaty, little snitch. "'I'm going to beat this fucking murder case'?"

"Yes," Dudley answered with more certainty. "He said that."

Brunelle smiled and set the report down on his table again. "Thank you. No further questions."

If Edwards had been angry before, she was livid after Brunelle ended his examination on that. She popped out of her seat, snatched her own copy of the report off her counsel table and marched right up to Dudley.

"Isn't it true Mr. Harris also said—"

"Objection," Brunelle interrupted. "Calls for hearsay."

That was true. If the prosecutor elicited what the defendant said about the crime, that was, by rule, not hearsay. Evidence Rule 801 said a statement made by an opponent is not hearsay, even if it otherwise would be. It was a useful rule in civil trials, for money, but it applied to criminal cases too. Which meant, if a defense attorney tried to elicit the exact same statement of her own client, it was still hearsay, and it wasn't admissible. Brunelle didn't make the rules, but he was going to enforce them. That's what he did for a living.

"Your Honor," Edwards complained up to Judge Parker, arms held wide. But she didn't have a response. Brunelle was right. He just needed her not to give up.

"Mr. Brunelle..." Judge Parker was able to put an obvious warning in the simple saying of his name. Like any judge, she didn't appreciate games in her courtroom. On the other hand, trials were really just one big game. "I think there may be some equitable concerns about admitting only the one sentence you elicited."

Brunelle had no doubt about that. But he needed the judge to rule based on the hearsay rules, not 'equitable concerns'.

"Perhaps if Ms. Edwards can articulate an exception to the hearsay rule," he suggested.

Practice around hearsay was all about the exceptions. Evidence Rule 802 said, 'Hearsay is not admissible except as provided by these rules.' It was that 'except' and those other rules that mattered. Evidence Rules 803 and 804 listed the exceptions. Every trial lawyer had at least some of those memorized. Dying declarations. Prior testimony. Family bibles. And the most commonly used one:

"Excited utterance!" Edwards called out on frustration. "The report said he was agitated and slapped the wall."

Evidence Rule 803. Exceptions to Rule Against Hearsay. The following are not excluded by the rule against hearsay:

(2) Excited Utterance. A statement relating to a startling event or condition, made while the declarant was under the stress of excitement that it caused.

"Mr. Brunelle?" Judge Parker asked.

"If Ms. Edwards can lay the foundation, Your Honor," he responded with a shrug.

Edwards huffed and stepped back directly in front of Dudley. "When Mr. Harris made these other statements about the murder of Ms. Carter, did he appear," she looked down again at Chen's crumpled report in her hands, "agitated and excited?"

"Um yes," Dudley replied, looking ever more frightened. "That sounds right."

"Did he also slap the wall?" Edwards demanded.

"Yes," Dudley answered. "I remember that."

"So, you would agree with me then," Edwards very definitely put the words from the rule in his mouth, "that Mr. Harris was under the stress of excitement caused by a startling event or condition?"

Dudley's brow knotted together. "Sure?"

Edwards threw her hands open to the judge again. "Excited utterance, Your Honor. The statements are admissible."

Judge Parker looked to Brunelle. "Any argument?"

Brunelle waited a moment, but only to try to sell it. He didn't wait two. "No, Your Honor."

"I will find the statements are excited utterances," Judge

Parker ruled, "and are admissible as exceptions to the hearsay rule. You may proceed, Ms. Edwards."

Brunelle sat down again and allowed himself to smile.

Carlisle bumped him. "Are you sure you know what you're doing?"

Brunelle nodded. He'd never been more sure.

While Edwards got Dudley to tell the jury about the rest of what Harris said, and specifically the statements, 'I didn't fucking kill her' and 'I was nowhere near her that night,' Brunelle opened his own copy of the evidence rules to Evidence Rule 806. He hadn't dared do it during the argument, lest Edwards see him and spy what was on the page. But once she had won the objection, the damage was done, and irrevocable.

The thing about the hearsay rule was that it was complicated, but not too complicated. Most lawyers mostly understood it. Brunelle's criminal procedure professor in law school had told his class, 'A third of you will understand this rule immediately. A third of you will understand it after we learn it. And a third of you will never fully understand it no matter how much we discuss it.' Even judges could get confused, especially when the hearsay statement being excluded was made by the same witness who was on the witness stand just then. But most trial attorneys developed a functional, if not perfect, grasp of it. Like any tasks, you got good at the parts you practiced the most. And there were parts that you weren't so good at because they almost never came up.

Every lawyer knew the exclusionary rule, ER 802. Most of them knew the most common exceptions under ER 803. A lot of them could give at least one example of the lesser used exceptions under ER 804. A few were familiar with the logic puzzle of 'hearsay within hearsay' addressed in ER 805. And almost none of them ever bothered to read ER 806. The rule Brunelle was about to shove right into the heart of Judge Parker's suppression ruling.

Edwards had finished, and Judge Parker asked Brunelle the standard, "Any redirect examination?"

"No, Your Honor." He stood up. "But I do have a motion."

CHAPTER 35

Judge Parker glared down at Brunelle but couldn't fully suppress a begrudging smile. Edwards wasn't smiling. If anything, she looked panicked. In part, because Brunelle looked so confident.

"I believe we need a recess anyway, Your Honor," Brunelle pointed out.

That was true. They needed the jurors to be hidden away again in the jury room while Dudley was re-handcuffed and escorted out of the courtroom.

Parker nodded, then turned to the jurors. "Ladies and gentlemen of the jury. I realize we just had a recess, but there is a matter I need to discuss with the lawyers outside of your presence. Please retire to the jury room, and the bailiff will come get you once we are ready for you again."

The jurors, being jurors, did as they were directed by the judge. After a few minutes, they were safely out of sight and hearing, Dudley was on his way back to the jail, and Judge Parker invited Brunelle to make the motion she probably realized was coming as soon as he announced his intention to make it.

"Thank you, Your Honor." He had remained standing while the jurors and the witness departed. He was too excited to sit down. But he did his best to appear calm and precise as he articulated what he wanted the judge to do. And why she had no choice but to do it. He was acutely aware of audience. Not just the judge, but the family seated behind him who had long ago lost faith in his ability to bring justice to them. There were others in the courtroom, random strangers stopping by to see The Justice System at work, but those were his two audiences. He needed to project confidence and competence. And he needed to win.

"The State moves to admit the defendant's confession to the police under Evidence Rule 806, Attacking and Supporting Credibility of Declarant."

"Are you kidding me?!" Edwards called out. She grabbed for her own evidence rules. "806? What are you talking about? Evidence rules don't trump the constitution."

Brunelle looked up at the judge. "May I continue?"

"You may," she answered. "Please don't interrupt again, Ms. Edwards. I will give you a chance to respond."

"Thank you, Your Honor," Brunelle said. "Evidence Rule 806 states very clearly, 'When a hearsay statement has been admitted in evidence, the credibility of the declarant may be attacked by any evidence which would be admissible for those purposes if declarant had testified as a witness.' The declarant here, of course, is the defendant. Ms. Edwards just had his statement to Mr. Dudley admitted as hearsay, under the excited utterance exception in ER 803. That means I am now allowed to attack Mr. Harris's credibility by any evidence that I could have used if he himself had actually taken the stand and testified as a witness. "

Brunelle took a moment to assess Edwards's reaction to his argument. She had a hand stuck in her hair, and her eyes were wide and glued to the evidence book in her other hand. That was all good, he thought. He continued.

"A suppression ruling does not give the defendant a license to lie," he reminded the judge. "Mr. Harris would not have been allowed to take the stand and claim he was not involved in the murder. Not without consequence. The suppression order prevented the State from offering the confession in its case-in-chief, but it was always the case that it would have been admitted as rebuttal evidence if the defendant chose to testify and said something different from what he told the police. We all understood that, and we all expected Mr. Harris would not testify in this trial for that very reason.

"But now, Your Honor, he has in effect testified, at least for the purposes of the evidence rules. Ms. Edwards, his attorney, solicited his statements, as hearsay, and those statements are to the jury as evidence in this case. The jury has heard Mr. Harris say, through Mr. Dudley, that he did not murder Ms. Carter and that he was not anywhere near her that day. I have evidence to attack the credibility of those statements, now that they have been made, and Evidence Rule 806 says I get to do that. This Court would not have hesitated to admit the confession to rebut live testimony by Mr. Harris that he was not the murderer, and it should not hesitate now to admit the confession to rebut the testimony of Mr. Harris which Ms. Edwards just provided the jury, over my objection, I might add."

"Not a very strenuous objection, I noted," Judge Parker remarked. "Although now I understand why." She turned to

Edwards. "Response?"

Edwards took a moment, then looked up from her evidence rules. The color had drained from her face. She had screwed up, and she knew it. So did the judge. It was really just a formality to allow her to argue against the oncoming freight train she had allowed herself to be tricked into unleashing.

"My response, Your Honor, is that this is not fair," she tried, returning to the notion of 'equitable concerns' when she could find no protection in the rules. "Mr. Brunelle manufactured evidence after the beginning of trial, then intentionally withheld only a portion of that evidence, leaving me with no choice but to seek admission of the remainder of the evidence."

"You could have left it at 'I'm going to beat this murder charge'," Judge Parker pointed out. "That's not necessarily an incriminating statement. It kind of sounds like what an innocent person might say."

"Perhaps," Edwards conceded, "but I can't just hope the jury will see it that way, can I? Not when there were further statements that clarified why he expected to beat the charge, namely that he didn't do it."

"But isn't that the problem, Ms. Edwards?" the judge asked. "The jury has now heard your client testify, essentially, that he didn't do it. That was done knowing full well that the State had statements by your client to the contrary. Why should the jury be left with only the statements that he didn't commit the murder, when he also stated that he did do it?"

"Because the Court suppressed those other statements," Edwards tried.

"I suppressed those statements because the officers didn't follow the rules," Judge Parker answered. "Explain to me why I shouldn't hold you to the same standard. They made a mistake, and the confession was suppressed. You just made a mistake, and I believe Mr. Brunelle is correct, the confession comes in now."

Edwards looked down again at her evidence rulebook, but she would find no solace there.

"Anything further?" the judge asked.

Brunelle considered asking the judge to allow the murder weapon to be admitted too. Harris did say he hadn't been there that night, and Amelia Carter's still wet blood was pretty good evidence to the contrary. But he decided not to get greedy.

Edwards looked over at Brunelle. "You're not calling Cooper to the stand, are you? You know he's a liar."

Brunelle shook his head. He took no pleasure in humiliating Edwards, but he wasn't going to lose the case either, if he could help it. "No, I'm going to call Jensen."

"He's a liar too," Edwards sneered.

"A recovering liar," Brunelle countered. "The lesser of two evils."

CHAPTER 36

Jensen was a liar, recovering or not. And Edwards would make absolutely sure the jury knew that. But Brunelle didn't have much of a choice. He needed the jury to hear what Harris had told the cops the night of the murder. Putting Jensen on was risky. But putting Cooper on would have been unethical.

He'd just have to be surgical about it. Avoid any testimony about doorways and warrants. Straight to the confession.

"Please state your name for the record," Brunelle began.

"Jeremy Jensen, sir," he answered.

One good thing was that Jensen seemed truly remorseful for his previous 'inaccurate' testimony. Ashamed even. It made him a docile and compliant witness.

"How are you employed?" Brunelle asked. He left off the 'for now'.

"I'm a police officer with the Seattle Police Department." That much was obvious from his uniform, but Brunelle needed it to be stated out loud for the record too. The appellate judges reviewing the case wouldn't see Jensen's navy blue jumpsuit and gold badge.

"Were you involved in the investigation of the murder of Amelia Carter?"

Jensen thought for a moment. "I was involved in the case, sir. I'm not sure I did any actual investigation myself."

"Fair enough," Brunelle allowed. "Did your involvement include contact with the defendant, Kevin Harris?"

Jensen looked over at the defendant, seated next to his still shellshocked lawyer. "Yes, sir."

"When did that contact occur, in relation to the murder?"

"We located and contacted Mr. Harris approximately one hour after the initial callout to the scene."

"The murder scene?" Brunelle wanted to clarify. He also wanted the jury to hear the word 'murder' again.

"Yes, sir."

"Where did you contact Mr. Harris?"

"At his residence, sir," Jensen answered. "A small house about a mile away from the victim's apartment."

Brunelle took a moment. He needed the confession in, and while Parker was allowing that, he also wanted to avoid any further discussion about the unconstitutionality of warrantless entries into people's homes. That might give Edwards fuel to try to fight one more time to keep the confession out.

"Eventually," Brunelle jumped over that unpleasantness, "did you hear the defendant make any statements about the murder?"

Jensen nodded. "Yes, sir." Brunelle knew Jensen had been trained at the academy to address all of his responses to the jury when testifying, but he was keeping his eyes on

Brunelle. Probably too ashamed to look at the jurors, Brunelle supposed.

"Did he make those statements to you or to other officers in your presence?"

Jensen considered. "I think he made them to both of us. I wasn't really the one asking the questions, but I was standing right there."

"Good enough." Brunelle responded. "Now, tell us. What did Mr. Harris tell the police one hour after the murder when he was contacted at his residence only a mile away?"

"Sure," Jensen agreed. He took a moment to gather his answer together. "He said that he used to be boyfriend/girlfriend with Ms. Carter. He said he went to her apartment that night because he was hoping to, um, maybe spend some time with her. Some intimate time."

"Understood," Brunelle interjected. "What else did he say?"

"He also said that he was hoping to maybe get some money or drugs from her, too, but when he got there, she wasn't happy to see him. He said they got into a verbal argument and then she slapped him. He said it escalated quickly, and he grabbed a knife from the kitchen knife block and stabbed her. He didn't know how many times exactly, but he said it was a lot. Then he said he fled to his home with the knife."

Brunelle nodded along with the recitation. He didn't want to get greedy, but the jury had just heard about the knife. He might as well ask.

"Did you happen to notice a knife with fresh blood on it anywhere in plain sight when you were at his residence?"

Brunelle braced for Edwards's objection, but it didn't come. He guessed that she figured it wouldn't have mattered at that point anyway.

"I believe the knife was visible inside the house, yes, sir," Jensen answered. "On the kitchen counter, I believe."

And Brunelle was done. He'd gotten the confession to the jury. He just needed to get out of the way and let the jury do their job. "No further questions," he informed the judge.

Judge Parker looked to Edwards. "Cross-examination?" she invited.

Edwards rose to her feet. "Oh, hell, yes," she said under her breath, although not so quietly that Brunelle didn't hear it.

She stormed forward to take a spot directly in front of Jensen, definitely a step or two too close to the witness stand. "You're a liar, aren't you, Officer Jensen?"

"Ma'am?" was all he could manage to respond.

"You're a liar," Edwards repeated. "You've lied about this case, haven't you? You came into this very courtroom, sat in that very chair in an earlier hearing and lied under oath about what happened that night when you and Sergeant Cooper arrested my client. Isn't that true?"

"Um, well." Jensen shifted in his seat. "I corrected my testimony."

"Because it was a lie," Edwards translated. "Right? First, you lied, but then you told the truth, right?"

"My first testimony was not perfectly accurate," Jensen tried. "I sought out the prosecutor and told him that. Then we had another hearing, and I corrected my testimony."

"So, again, you lied," Edwards translated, "but then you felt bad about it and changed your testimony."

"Corrected," Jensen insisted.

"And the thing you lied about," Edwards pressed forward, "was the contact you had with my client that very night, exactly when he allegedly made this confession. Isn't that right?"

Jensen considered for a moment. "The testimony I corrected was about our contact with the defendant that night, yes."

"So, you have previously lied, under oath, about the very thing you just testified about again."

Jensen waited a moment, then asked, "Is that a question, ma'am?"

"Here's a question for you, Officer Jensen." Edwards leaned in even closer to the witness. "Given that you have already lied at least once about your contact with my client that night, why should this jury or anyone else ever believe anything you have to say about that?"

Jensen accepted the question with a nod, then looked down for several seconds. When he looked up, all he could do was shrug. "Because now I'm telling the truth, ma'am."

Edwards's sneer turned into a full-blown scowl. "Sounds exactly like what a liar would say. No further questions."

She spun on her heel and marched back to her seat next to Harris. She looked beyond angry. Harris looked scared.

"Any redirect?" Judge Parker asked.

"No, Your Honor," Brunelle answered, standing to do so.

"Any further witnesses for the State?" the judge followed up.

Brunelle looked down to his co-counsel to confirm. Carlisle shook her head.

"No, Your Honor," Brunelle answered. "The State rests."

CHAPTER 37

Edwards wouldn't even look at Brunelle when the judge adjourned early for the day, and the week, giving Edwards three full days to prepare for how, or whether, to put on a case. She also didn't answer when Brunelle called her office that afternoon. Three times.

So he was pleasantly surprised when he reached his car that night to find a small envelope tucked under his windshield wiper with a note from Edwards inside:

We need to talk.

Meet me at the Rat City Tavern, Beacon Hill.

8:00 p.m. Come alone.

~Jessica

That last bit was weird, but Brunelle supposed Edwards might still be embarrassed by what happened that day. He was just glad for the opportunity to talk it through. Especially over drinks.

He looked at his watch. 6:37. Enough time to swing by his place and change. Not that he minded wearing a suit as a general proposition, even until the end of the day, but the 'Rat City

Tavern' didn't sound like the kind of place where a lot of people would be wearing suits. And besides, it had been a stressful day. He'd pretty much sweated through his suit.

CHAPTER 38

Brunelle had never been to the Rat City Tavern before, so he had to rely on his phone's GPS. He found it slightly concerning that his phone flagged it as currently 'closed' but he supposed maybe it was one of those dive bars that opened late. That would explain why Edwards wanted to meet at eight o'clock instead of right after work.

The GPS led him up Beacon Avenue, past the businesses on the main drag, then a right on Winthrop and a left on Twelfth. He would have gone farther, but the road ended against the 20-foot-tall concrete wall that separated the neighborhood from the drop-off to Interstate 5, dampening at least some of the constant din from the unrelenting current of cars below.

And there, across from the sound wall, tucked under some overgrown trees that blocked most of the light of the only nearby streetlamp was the entrance to the Rat City Tavern.

It looked very closed. Out of business closed. There were no other businesses nearby, no foot traffic, and no other cars, save one. Edwards's car. She was there, leaning against her car looking at her phone. He was in the right place after all.

Brunelle parked at the corner, a few spots back from Edwards's car, and stepped out into the cool evening.

"Jess?" he called out.

"Dave," she called back, lowering her phone and looking his way. "Why the hell did you want to meet at this—?"

Two gunshots rang out. Edwards flew backwards and fell to the ground, her phone skittering away on the pavement.

Brunelle instinctively dropped into a crouch next to his car. "Jess?" he called out again. "Are you okay?"

She didn't answer.

But someone else did.

"No, Dave. She's not okay. And it's all your fault."

Brunelle turned toward the voice and watched as a man stepped out from the shadows under the trees by the wall. He cut across the street at an angle, along the far side of Brunelle's car, and placed himself directly between Brunelle and Edwards's motionless body. Brunelle had changed clothes, but this man was wearing a suit and tie. And gloves. And holding a handgun in each hand: one by the barrel, the other pointed directly at Brunelle.

Brunelle didn't recognize him particularly—it had been seventeen years, and he didn't get a good look at him at the liquor store—but he knew who he was. "Larson."

"Nice to see you again, Mr. Brunelle," Larson replied. "It's been a long time. Well, not really. I saw you in court today. Seated in the back row. You did an excellent job, but I don't think you noticed me. It's amazing how a middle-aged white man in a suit just sort of melts into the scenery at a courthouse. Everyone assumed I was just another lawyer, when in reality—"

"You're a murderer," Brunelle finished for him. He

looked past Larson at Edwards's body sprawled out on the pavement. "Twice."

"Oh, no, Mr. Brunelle. I didn't kill Jessica Edwards." He held up the gun he was holding by the barrel. "You did." He set it on the ground, out of reach of Brunelle, but lined up between his car and Edwards.

"My gun," Brunelle knew. "From my car."

Larson nodded. "Yes. I wasn't just trying to scare you, Mr. Brunelle. There was a method to my madness. When the police arrive, they will find you, and your gun, and the defense attorney you had a very public dispute with in court today."

"I'm pretty sure they'll take my word over yours, Larson," Brunelle responded. He was still crouching, but his legs were protesting greatly. He slowly pushed himself to his feet.

"I'm sure they would," Larson agreed, "if that's all the evidence there was. But in Ms. Edwards's pocket the police will find the invitation I left on Ms. Edwards's windshield, signed by you."

"You don't know what my signature looks like, Larson," Brunelle answered. "That will just prove it wasn't me."

Larson laughed. "Your signature is available on thousands of public documents, Mr. Brunelle. Every legal pleading you've ever filed. It wasn't difficult to forge the word 'Dave'. But more importantly, the envelope seal has your DNA on it."

Brunelle's brow creased. That would be more troubling. "How?"

"You probably didn't notice among the rest of the carnage when I visited your home," Larson grinned, his teeth a dull silver in the streetlight, "but I took your toothbrush. It was a simple matter of wetting it to seal the envelope."

Brunelle reached for the envelope in his own pocket.

"I used it to seal your invitation as well." Larson noted Brunelle's motion. "So, if you show the police that to prove your innocence, they'll just think you set up an alibi in advance. That's premeditation, Mr. Brunelle. Murder in the first degree. You're going to die in prison."

"This won't work, Larson," Brunelle asserted, although he was beginning to suspect it just might.

"I even dropped the receipt from the liquor store—the one with your credit card number on it—on the ground on the other side of your car right now." Larson was clearly pleased with his own cleverness. "Just in case you managed to get away before the cops got here. But listen, the police are already on their way."

Sure enough, there were already sirens in the distance.

"I fired twice to make sure the neighbors would hear and know it was gunfire," Larson went on. "Well, that, and we both know, if you're going to kill someone, you fire two shots, center mass. I learned that in prison, Mr. Brunelle. I learned a lot in prison. I had a lot of time to think about how I was going to kill you. But then I realized it wasn't enough. I needed to do to you what you did to me. You didn't kill me, but you took my life from me. And now I'm taking yours away the same way."

"When the cops get here, I'll tell them who I am," Brunelle tried to sound confident. "They'll believe me. Hell, they probably know me."

"Oh, they'll know you, Mr. Brunelle. I'm sure of that." Larson's unsettling grin broadened. "I didn't pick this location just because it was abandoned and isolated. I picked it because it's the same sector as Amelia Carter's apartment."

The sirens suddenly became much louder and red and blue lights flashed against the concrete of the sound wall.

"Goodbye, Mr. Brunelle." Larson stepped back into the shadows as the patrol cars came screeching around the corner and surrounded Brunelle. "Say hello to Sergeant Cooper for me."

CHAPTER 39

Larson was right. It was Cooper who reached Brunelle first, the on-duty sector sergeant leading the response to a call of shots fired. He leaped from his car, gun drawn, and drove Brunelle's face into the pavement. When he realized who his perp was, he let out a belly laugh of purest glee. He was only too happy to handcuff Brunelle too tightly, yank his shoulder out of the socket to get him to his feet, and throw him in the back of his patrol cruiser, not quite lowering his head enough to avoid banging it off the doorframe. Brunelle sincerely wondered whether he'd actually make it to the jail, or might instead end up in a ditch somewhere with a Seattle Police Department-issued slug in the back of his head. But for some people, there was joy in the humiliation of others, and Cooper was beyond ecstatic to march Brunelle into the King County Jail and book him in on suspicion of murder in the first degree.

Brunelle didn't know every corrections officer at the jail, but he knew a few, and even more knew him. The bad news was the additional humiliation of his fall from ally to prisoner. The good news was, they knew not to put him in general population. After being photographed, fingerprinted, and dressed out in orange jail scrubs, Brunelle found himself alone in a distressingly bright 10-foot by 10-foot concrete cell. He didn't even get to make a phone call.

Brunelle sat down on the metal shelf bolted to the wall that was supposed to serve as a bed. The only other places to sit were the seatless metal toilet or the floor. He lowered his head into his hands and tried to tell himself it was going to be all right. Surely all of his friends in the police and the courts would know it was a setup. That he could never have done something like that. Especially not to Edwards. Not Jess.

"Oh fuck," he exhaled. He'd forgotten. Edwards was dead. "Oh my God, she's dead."

The cell door clanked loudly and swung open. Brunelle looked up to see the one person in law enforcement he knew he could trust. Well, one of two, assuming Emory was going to stand by him. Which she would. Probably.

"Dave." Chen stood in the doorway, expression dour, an armed corrections officer visible behind him.

"Larry!" Brunelle jumped to his feet, but Chen put out a hand to stop him from getting closer.

"I've called Casey," he said.

"Thank you," Brunelle answered.

"I assume you don't want to answer any questions right now?" Chen suggested.

In truth, the only thing Brunelle wanted to do at that moment was to tell them what really happened. But he also knew Chen was right. Remain silent. But he finally, viscerally, understood why so many suspects fell all over themselves to give up that constitutional right and try to convince the cops of their innocence.

"Um, right," Brunelle agreed. "I guess I need a lawyer."

Chen nodded. "Good idea. But it won't be until the morning. Before you go to court."

Court. Oh fuck. It was real. He was going to be charged with murder. He was going to go to court, and the judge was going to set bail, and he was going to get a public defender because he was absolutely, certainly, one-hundred-percent going to be fired.

"Here." Chen extended a hand, holding a worn paperback. "It's the best I can do right now. Read a book."

Brunelle hesitated, then accepted the gift and read the title aloud. "*Escape from Mars.* Uh, thanks. I mean, I'm not really a sci-fi fan, though."

Chen didn't quite manage to suppress a roll of his eyes. "Then skim it. Read the first paragraph of each chapter. You can even skip the odd ones."

"Um, okay." That was weird advice. But he forced a smile and slapped the cover of the book. "Thanks, Larry."

Chen nodded at the 'bed'. "Get some rest. You've got a big morning coming up."

"A big day," Brunelle replied.

Chen closed his eyes and let out a small sigh. "Goodbye, Dave."

Chen stepped back out of the doorway, and the guard slammed the cell door shut again, sending a metallic echo through the concrete room.

Brunelle looked at the book again. *Escape from Mars.*

Too bad he wasn't on Mars. There was no escape for him.

CHAPTER 40

It was dark when Brunelle's cell door clanked open again, waking him from a restless sleep on the cold metal of his new bed.

He squinted up at the figure backlit by the light spilling in from the hallway.

"Get up." It was Chen. "Let's go."

Brunelle wasn't going to argue. He rolled off his bed and followed Chen out of the cell. Chen handcuffed him, then pushed him in front of him. "Walk."

Again, no argument, but he was curious what was happening. It was definitely too early for morning court. He hadn't been asleep for more than a couple of hours.

Chen pushed him forward, down several corridors, through some doors, and down a flight of stairs. A few more secure doors later, opened with Chen's key card, and they were standing on the loading docks off the back of the jail.

Emory's car was waiting.

"What's going on?" Brunelle asked from the back seat once they were all safely inside the car.

Chen turned around to uncuff him. "Did you read the book like I told you?"

Brunelle shook his head. "No. I told you. I don't like sci-fi."

Chen shook his head and faced forward again. "There was a code, you idiot. The first paragraph of each even chapter had one word underlined. It said, 'We know. We have a plan. Stay awake. Be ready.'"

Brunelle rubbed his wrists again. He was getting tired of being handcuffed. "Wow. Very cloak and dagger."

"We didn't want you to panic and try to kill yourself or something," Emory explained as she drove toward the Twelfth Avenue Bridge.

"Well, that's nice," Brunelle supposed. "But I would have taken my chances with the system."

"The system thinks you're a prosecutor who snapped and murdered a defense attorney," Emory responded. "You're the biggest story on the news right now, and you've pretty much already been convicted. At least we know why he took your gun."

"Well, see, you can testify about that," Brunelle said. "You can tell everyone my gun was stolen weeks before the murder."

"Your girlfriend?" Emory laughed. "And I didn't see the theft. I could only say that's what you said happened. Just more evidence of premeditation."

"My girlfriend, huh?" Brunelle grinned. "So, you'd stand by even if I were accused of murder?"

"You are accused of murder." Emory shook her head. Then, after a moment, "And yes. I'm standing by you."

"Well, that's nice." Brunelle leaned back in his seat.

"Also, Edwards isn't dead," Chen informed him.

"What? Really?" Brunelle shot back upright. "He missed?"

"No, two shots, center mass," Chen confirmed. "But she was wearing a ballistic vest."

"A bulletproof vest?" Brunelle was more than a little surprised. "To meet me? Did she think I was going to shoot her? Why would I do that? I won the motion."

"She believed you," Emory explained. "When you warned her about Larson. She contacted S.P.D., and they provided her with a vest and a panic button in her house."

Brunelle frowned. "How come I didn't get that?"

"You never asked," Chen answered.

Brunelle thought for a moment. "How do you know all that? Did you talk to her?"

"Yeah, she's at Harborview Hospital," Chen explained. "It still hurts like hell when you get shot, and she hit her head when she fell. It knocked her out, but she'll be okay."

Brunelle thought for a moment. "Well, this is great. She can say I didn't shoot her."

But Chen and Emory both shook their heads.

"She didn't see who shot her," Chen said.

"She only saw you," Emory added.

"Ooh," Brunelle responded. "That's not good."

"No, not good," Emory agreed. "Victim I.D.s you as the only person there, your gun, and a note from you telling her to meet you there."

"That note is a forgery," Brunelle pointed out.

"I figured as much," Emory answered.

"But it is my DNA on the envelope," he added.

"What?" Chen turned to look back at him.

"Larson stole my toothbrush when he trashed my condo," Brunelle explained. "He told me he used it to seal the envelope so my DNA would be on it like I licked it myself."

"He's good," Emory observed.

"Well, he had a lot of time to plan it," Brunelle said. "Speaking of plans, what's ours? I assume you're not aiding my escape by driving me to Canada."

"Um, no," Emory confirmed. "I'm sticking by you, but I'm not rendering you criminal assistance. I like my job. And my freedom."

"Me too," Brunelle said. "So how are we going to save them?"

"There's too much evidence against you right now," Chen said. "You go to trial on the evidence they have—"

"Plus the DNA," Emory added.

"Plus the DNA," Chen agreed, "and you're going down on murder."

"Well, attempted murder," Brunelle corrected, "but still. Bad."

"Yes. Bad," Emory agreed.

"So, your only hope is more evidence," Chen reasoned. "New evidence."

"Like what?"

Chen smiled and looked out the windshield. "You're not going to like it."

* * *

A few minutes later, they were parked three blocks up from the defunct Rat City Tavern, the crime scene's yellow cordon fluttering slightly in the pre-dawn streetlight.

"Explain this to me one more time," Brunelle said as he changed out of his jail jammies and into the outfit Chen and

Emory had brought him.

"I had our Public Information Officer plant a fake story in the media last night," Chen explained. "He told them that there were some discrepancies at the crime scene that might cast doubt on the identity of the shooter, and further investigation would commence in the morning."

"Well, that's good news," Brunelle said.

"No, Dave." Emory shook her head. "It's not true."

"Our only hope is that Larson shows up again tonight to try to clean up whatever mistake he thinks he made."

"He didn't make any mistakes," Brunelle said.

"Yeah, but he doesn't know that," Chen replied. "Not for sure. And he's come too far to let this slip through his fingers."

"Okay, then what?"

"Then..." Emory started, but she stopped and pointed down the street. "Someone's there."

Brunelle squinted down the street. There appeared to be a dark figure at the edge of the crime tape. "Are you sure?"

"Yes," Emory answered. "Now go."

Brunelle took a deep breath, then pulled on the door handle and pushed himself out of the car.

Stay calm, Dave, he told himself. *You're just sneaking up on a homicidal maniac in the middle of the night. What could possibly go wrong?*

But Brunelle knew it had to be him who confronted Larson. Anyone else, and Larson would have some excuse for being there. And not something stupid like he was lost or looking for a quarter he dropped. He'd tell them the truth. He heard about that prosecutor who got arrested for murder, and that same prosecutor convicted him of murder years ago, so he was curious and wanted to see the scene. The best lies are mostly true.

There was only one person who that lie wouldn't work on.

"Hello, Jacob," Brunelle said when he reached the yellow police tape, his enemy already several feet inside the crime scene.

Larson spun around. "You! What are you doing here? How are you even here?"

"It's over, Jacob," Brunelle said as calmly as he could, hands in his pockets, trying to look confident despite knowing Larson undoubtedly had that second gun on him. "It didn't work."

Larson swung his head around the crime scene. "It had to work. I did everything right."

"You're a loser, Jacob," Brunelle provoked him. "Just like you were the first time I sent you to prison. A loser, and a coward, and a murderer."

But Larson shook an agitated finger at Brunelle. "No, no, no. You may have friends who helped you post bail or something, but that doesn't mean they won't charge you. That doesn't mean you're not going to prison for murder."

"You messed up, Jacob," Brunelle continued. He ducked under the crime scene tape and took a step toward Larson. "You missed something."

Larson took a step back and put his own hand in his coat pocket. Brunelle knew what was in there. He hoped Chen and Emory were following up on their part of the plan. "No, I thought of everything."

"Not everything." Brunelle took another step toward him.

"Your gun. Your DNA. Your enemy." Larson took

another step backward. Then he extracted that second gun and leveled it at Brunelle. "I planned it perfectly."

But Brunelle shook his head. "That was your mistake, Jacob. Jess is my opponent. She's not my enemy."

Brunelle looked vaguely over his shoulder at the shadows surrounding him and Larson. "Is that enough?" he called out.

Larson's eyes darted around the dark scene.

"I really hope that's enough," Brunelle called out again.

"I guess it will have to be," Chen stepped out of the shadows, followed by Emory. They both had their firearms locked on Larson. "Not a perfectly clear-cut confession, but the context fills in the gaps."

Larson looked from Brunelle to the approaching detectives and back to Brunelle again. "No. No, no, no. I didn't admit to anything. I just said it was your gun and that's true, it was."

"You also said it was my DNA," Brunelle reminded him, "which is a weird thing to know, right? And also, that you planned it. That'll be enough evidence. I could convict you of murder on that. I mean, convict you of murder *again*."

"Lower your weapon, Larson." Chen took a step toward him as Emory lined up a clear shot. "You're under arrest for the attempted murder of Jessica Edwards."

Larson's eyes flared, but he kept the gun trained on Brunelle's chest. "Attempted? She's alive?"

"Yeah, dummy," Brunelle taunted. "You missed."

Larson looked at Chen, then Emory, then back to Brunelle. He knew it was over. But he smiled. "I won't miss again."

Two shots, center mass.

Brunelle felt the shots almost before he heard them. He fell backward on the pavement, his head whiplashing into the concrete as his body went limp. But he didn't lose consciousness. He heard the volley of shots that followed and the sound of Larson's own body falling to the ground, undoubtedly riddled by bullets from Chen's and Emory's weapons.

Brunelle couldn't move. The pain in his chest radiated down his left arm and both of his legs. After a moment, he could hear Chen radioing for backup, and Emory came over and knelt next to him. She ran a hand over where the bullets had struck him, placed her other hand on his face, and looked him deeply in the eyes.

"Dave, honey?"

"Yes, darling?" he gasped, staring up at her angelic face.

"Get the hell up." She slapped his chest. "The vest held. You're fine."

EPILOGUE

Under the circumstances, Judge Parker pushed closing arguments back a day. Edwards managed to give hers after downing about a dozen aspirin. Brunelle let Carlisle deliver theirs. Once Brunelle got the confession in, the verdict wasn't really in doubt. Guilty as charged, murder in the first degree. Premeditated intent only required more than a moment in time. There were a lot of moments in time between eleven stab wounds.

Brunelle ran into Edwards a few weeks later in the attorney lounge. Mercifully, she was alone, no defense courtiers to encourage her lesser impulses.

"Nice job on that trial," she offered. She was pouring a cup of coffee from the coffee maker. "It stung at the time, and I'm still mad at myself for not seeing what you were doing, but I can appreciate good advocacy. Even when I'm on the receiving end of it."

"Thanks," Brunelle said. "You know, I told Larson we were opponents but not enemies."

Edwards smiled and gave a little shrug. "For now." She

handed Brunelle the cup of coffee she'd just poured. "Let's see what happens in our next trial."

END

Made in United States
North Haven, CT
07 April 2022

18004545R00137